HELLHOUND'S SACRIFICE

SATAN'S KEEPERS MC BOOK 4

E.C. LAND

CONTENTS

Acknowledgments	ix
Trigger Warning	xiii
Playlist	xv
Satan's Keepers MC	xvii
Love's Sacrifice	xix
Prologue	1
Chapter 1	9
Chapter 2	17
Chapter 3	24
Chapter 4	33
Chapter 5	40
Chapter 6	49
Chapter 7	56
Chapter 8	61
Chapter 9	72
Chapter 10	77
Chapter 11	85
Chapter 12	91
Chapter 13	97
Chapter 14	106
Chapter 15	113
Chapter 16	117
Chapter 17	123
Chapter 18	128
Epilogue	134

Author's Note	139
War	141
Breathing in Sin	143
Inheriting Trouble	145
Remaining Gunner's	147
Also by E.C. Land	149
Coming Soon	155
Social Media	157

To those who feel they're never good enough . . . know you are.

ACKNOWLEDGMENTS

My Husband – For years, he's worked himself to death to give our family everything we needed or wanted. He encourages me every day to follow my dreams just like he did the day he told me to take the chance. He's my best friend, and I wouldn't know what to do without him. Or the fact he listens to my non-stop rambling or my always having a notepad with me in case I need to write something down that pops into my head.

My Three Kiddos – Every day, I watch them grow up into little people who want to take over the world. Well, in their own way, that is. They are inspirations all by themselves. They love to find out what I'm working on and give me ideas. One of my favorite things is to ask them what I should have someone do or how they should act. Some of their ideas are wicked.

My Alphas – You guys rock big time! Thank you all for being the first to read the stories as they come alive. It means the world to me. Especially when you all start to get mad, that's when I know I'm doing something right. And in doing so, pushing me to keep going with all the different plots that form in my head. I'm thankful to you all for being ready and willing to read and give your input.

My Knox Publishing People – Thank you guys for being such great people to work with.

Liz – My sister from another mister, my best friend, and Publisher/Boss/Co-Writer extraordinaire. You're my go-to when I need it. I love working with you on all that we do. No matter how much chaos we go through to get it done.

Diane – If not for you, I swear I would lose my head. You set me straight when I don't know which way to look. Thank you for everything you do in being the best PA I could ask for. However, you're also one amazing friend.

My Editing/Plotting Team – Thank you all for working with me. I truly do enjoy working alongside you all as I bring each and every book to life. I don't know what I would do without each and every one of you to help me when I need it most.

H̲e̲l̲l̲h̲o̲u̲n̲d̲'s̲ S̲a̲c̲r̲i̲f̲i̲c̲e̲

This book is a work of fiction. The names, characters, places, and incidents are all products of the author's imagination and are not to be construed as real. Any resemblances to persons, organizations, events, or locales are entirely coincidental.

Hellhound's Sacrifice. Copyright © 2022 by E.C. Land. All rights reserved. No part of this book may be used or reproduced in any manner whatsoever without written permission from the author, except in the case of brief quotations used in articles or reviews. For information, contact E.C. Land.

Cover Design by Clarise Tan, CT Cover Creations

Editing by Kim Lubbers

Formatting by E.C. Land

Proofreading by Anna Gorman

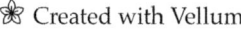 Created with Vellum

TRIGGER WARNING

This content is intended for mature audiences only. It contains material that may be viewed as offensive to some readers, including graphic language, dangerous and sexual situations, murder, rape, and extreme violence.

Proceed with caution. This book does entail several scenes that may very well be a trigger to some.

Also, tissues are a must with other scenes.

Not for the faint at heart.

If you don't like violence and cannot handle certain subjects, then this is not a book you'll want to read.

**Check out the playlist for
Hellhound's Sacrifice!**

Seeing Red – State of Mine
Reckless – Seth Anthony
Alone – I Prevail
Breaking Me Down – WHO TF IS JUSTIN TIME & Jesse Howard
Only if I Could – Nu Breed & Jesse Howard
Can't Be Me – Sean Stemaly
The Long Ride Home – Chase Matthew
Undeniable – Seckond Chaynce
Dancing With Your Ghost – No Resolve
I Don't Wanna Go To Heaven – Nate Smith
Fading Away – Sean Stemaly
Don't Be Stupid – Nu Breed & Jesse Howard
Burn it Down – Warren Zeiders

SATAN'S KEEPERS MC

O – OL' LADY & C – CHILD

Reaper – Prez — Ivy – O
Angel – VP
Hellhound – Sergeant At Arms — Isabelle – O
Daemon – Road Captain
Hendrik – C
Scythe – Tech
Tombstone – Enforcer — Sutton – O
Harvester - Treasurer
Thanatos - Chaplain
Styxx - Secretary
Beast - Member
Ghost - Member
Diablo - Member
Ghoul - Prospect
Goblin - Prospect

LOVE'S SACRIFICE

Red stains my hands
Nothing can take it away
Soap and water can't hide it
Blood coats them
But it also surrounds me
Tainting what one once was
Love is a sacrifice
One that will be good or bad
There are only two roads to take
The one that leads to redemption
And the one for despair
Sacrifice for those you love
Or turn your back and let them go
Red stains my hands
For love is what I sacrifice

PROLOGUE

HELLHOUND

Fifteen Years Ago – Age 20

Breathing heavily, I narrow my gaze to slits, staring at the man on the ground as he bleeds. His blood puddling under him, coating the grass as it does my hands.

"Asher," Stella calls my name, her voice trembling in fear.

I slowly tilt my head in her direction and meet her gaze. I take in the tears running down her face. The torn dress she'd been wearing when she left the house. I also note the blood also staining her skin.

I don't say anything. I can't. My entire body hurts,

and I've got to finish handling this situation before I can take care of myself.

"Please, Asher, say something . . . anything," Stella cries, trying to hold her dress together to keep herself covered.

I don't say anything, but I do strip off my cut and shirt. I hand my tee to Stella and put my cut back on. I reach into my pocket and grasp my cell phone, flipping it open. I go to my contacts and find the number I'm looking for, and hit the call button.

"Yeah," Reaper answers on the third ring.

I turn away from my sister and close my eyes. I only just got my patch with the club, and this is not what I was to be doing. Reaper took over being Prez a couple of years ago, and he's good at what he does.

"I need help, Prez." I hate having to ask, but right now, I need my brothers. They're the only ones I trust at the moment. If the cops are called, I'll be locked up, and there's no way in hell I'm about to go down for gutting a rapist.

"Right, where are you?" Reaper demands. In the background, I can hear movement and know he's on the move.

I give him the address and hang up. I need to start getting shit gathered together for when my brothers get here. We've got to get rid of the body and all evidence of what happened here.

"Asher, please, talk to me. I love you, you're my big

brother, and I can't stand the thought of you being mad at me. I should have listened to you," Stella cries and touches my shoulder.

I shrug off her touch and turn on her with anger in my eyes. "I've got nothing to say to you right now. I fuckin' warned you, and you didn't listen to me. You're a fuckin' Ryan, and you knew better. Mom and Dad raised you better than this. Now because of you and your stupidity for not listening to me, I'll remember this shit every time I look in the mirror," I snarl, pointing at my face where it hurts the most. I feel the blood running down my face and know it's sliced open. It's the only time the fucker got close enough to take the knife to me. In the end, I used the same knife on him, sinking it into his chest repeatedly.

"I'm sorry, Asher," Stella sobs. Her hands cover her mouth, and she shakes her head. "I screwed up, and I'm so, so, sorry."

"You're sorry? Grow the fuck up, then," I snarl and jerk my chin to the side. "Go stand over there and wait until I get this shit taken care of. Then your ass is on the first plane out of here. You're going to Ireland."

I've been watching my sister since our parents died after I turned eighteen. Stella is nearly that age now, but I'm done. She can go live with our uncle and cousins there until she goes to college.

I can't do this anymore. Because she didn't listen to me when I told her to come home after school, she went to a damn party she had no business being at. Then she calls me drunkenly, crying, wanting me to come get her. She gave me an address, but it was to some warehouse building. I don't even want to know what the hell was in her head. I'll forever remember it because it's now seared in my mind. I showed up just as the motherfucker was raping my sister, holding a knife to her throat.

I love my sister, but I'm done. She needs to grow up and learn to stop being as fuckin' selfish as she is. I've sacrificed, and she doesn't know what all I did to keep her with me, and this is the thanks I get. A scar that I'll never be able to forget. It will be there taunting me for the rest of my life as it reminds me of how much I failed at protecting my sister and the blood that now stains my hands.

ISABELLE

Ten Years Ago – Age 16

"Finally, I'm home," I sigh, thankful to be off work, granted home is no better. I can at least go to sleep for a couple of hours before getting up and ready for school.

Tomorrow being the weekend, I'll go to Everleigh's

and be able to relax with her and the rest of our friends. We're supposed to be going out to one of the ATV trials to have some fun. I can't wait. It's going to be a blast.

I just have to get through the rest of this night first. Then I'm free—for the time being.

Stepping into the house, I immediately regret coming home. Inside, my parents are both strung out of their minds, and their dealer, Dexter, is sitting with them. I should have known he'd be here. It's been a month, and he always comes to collect.

My parents aren't like others. My mom doesn't bake cookies in the oven or hold me while I cry over a boy calling me names. My dad doesn't teach me to defend myself or take me to father-daughter dinners. No, my parents are junkies and only care about their next fix. They've been this way my whole life.

In the past year, it's gotten worse. Dexter comes to collect on a monthly basis. He does this by giving my parents what they want, and they depend on me to pay. I learned to give in and do as I'm told because after the first time I refused to do so, their dealer didn't go at them. He came after me. I was a virgin, and he raped me. I ended up going to a free clinic for help because not only did he do that, but he also beat me to a bloody pulp. I was barely able to walk afterward.

I learned, and I've dealt with it since. My friends

don't know the depths of it all, but they do know about the majority of it.

My parent's dealer lifts his gaze to mine and grins while he appraises me as if I were a piece of meat.

"Do you have my money?" Dexter asks gruffly, keeping that smirk in place.

I swallow nervously and nod, hoping that the money will be enough. I don't just work one job after school. I have two. Both are barely enough to keep everything afloat. If it weren't for the fact that the rent is so cheap and my parents having food stamps, I'd be screwed. The light bill is the main thing that really hits me hard. I'm supposed to be a kid still making mistakes, not being an adult trying to manage everything.

"I suggest you go get it then," he states, licking his bottom lip, that knowing glint showing in his eyes as he stands.

Nodding, I quickly march down the hall, knowing he's following.

I step into my room and go straight to the drawer where I keep the money. I open it only to find it all missing.

"Where's my money, Isa?"

I cringe as his front comes flush with my back.

"I–I . . . th–they . . . must've taken it." Tears well in my eyes as I know what comes next.

Dexter chuckles deviously and grips both my arms.

"Well, then it looks like you're mine for the weekend, then Isa."

I find myself shoved further into the room. I stumble and fall onto my bed that sits on the floor. My eyes go to Dexter to find him leering at me.

"Get ready, baby. I've been looking forward to my time with you," he smirks, closing the door.

I inwardly send a prayer that I survive the weekend and hope one day I'll be free of this horrible life I live.

CHAPTER 1

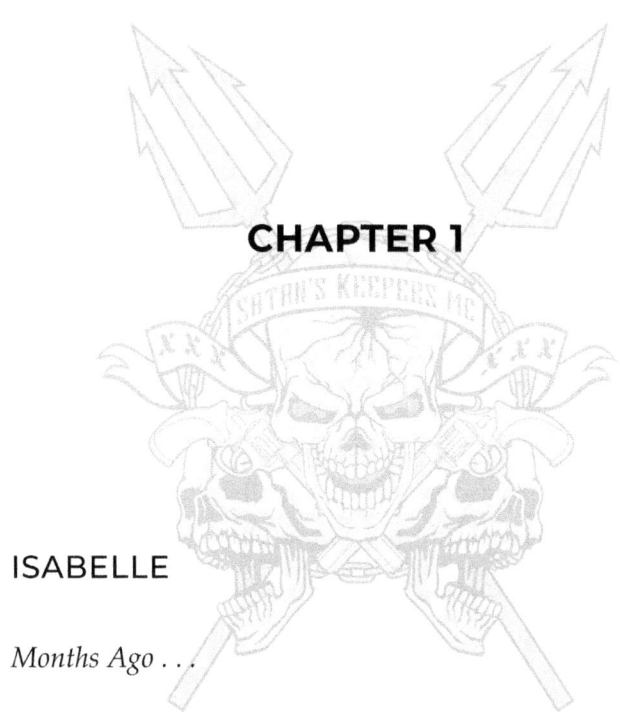

ISABELLE

Months Ago . . .

I rush into the hospital, spotting Sutton and the rest of my girls standing down the hall huddled together. My heart thuds against my chest, seeing the worried expressions on their faces. Not far down from them stands a group of seriously hot guys. Honestly, they're the hottest men I've ever seen, even with grim faces.

Sutton and Everleigh spot me first and take in my outfit—baggie long sleeve shirt, leggings, and my hair down. Juniper and Josephine notice me seconds after they do. Juniper opens her mouth to say something, but Sutton pinches her arm to hush her up. They know I don't want anyone to know.

A few of the men eye me as I stop near Sutton and give her a hug. The one that has a scar running down the side of his face catches my eye, and he seems to assess me momentarily before he turns away. Another one standing close to him is also looking in our direction, but I can't tell if he's looking at me or one of the others. It doesn't matter if he is. I know it would be me. I'm the ugly one out of our group. Hell, I've never even had a boyfriend, for that matter.

I pull away from Sutton and take a step back, curling my arms around my waist. "How is she?" I ask, worrying about our other friend Ivy. We're all best friends, more like family than anything.

"Reaper said she'll be okay," Sutton murmurs, nodding her head in the direction of the men. "He's heading to Ivy's room now and said he'd let us see her after he does."

Reaper is Ivy's man. She met him a little while ago and ironically spent a night with him before she knew Reaper was her new boss. They ended up together, and from the grim looks on all the men's faces standing around, the rest of them must really care for my friend.

I nod and focus on her rather than the men, not hiding the fact. They're taking us all in. "That's good."

"Yeah, but what about you?" Everleigh murmurs, grabbing hold of my wrists. She pushes my sleeve up and winces at the gruesome bruises on my skin. "It's getting worse." The way her brows crease in the middle of her forehead deepens when I yank my hand away.

"Babe," Sutton whispers, but I shake my head.

"No, don't. I . . . I was short this month. It won't happen again. I'll make sure of it. I have to. It just means I work harder and ask my boss for more hours. I'm sure she'll give them to me," I reassure them, wrapping my arms around my waist. "I've got this."

What my friends don't know is that my boss isn't the same one I had, considering they think I'm still a receptionist. I haven't told them I left my old job nearly a year ago and have been working well over an hour away in a strip club. I didn't want to take the chance of working at any of the clubs closer to home. There's no way in hell I'd want anyone I know to see me on stage. The last thing I need is for anything to get back to Dexter. He'd for sure raise his price on my parents, and I wouldn't have anything to my name, period. In the time I've started working at Hellfire Dancers, life's been marginally easier than it has in years.

They all look at me, ready to call me on my bullshit. Dexter decided to up his prices on the smack he sells, it's not the first time, and of course, my parents didn't pay. They never do. I didn't know he came calling to collect. I'd gotten good at making sure I had more than enough each time he found me. But that doesn't mean there aren't times I don't. For instance, these past two days. Thankfully Dexter wasn't able to do anything else but beat me. It's been that way for about two years now. I think it has to do with the amount of alcohol and the fact he's doing his own drugs—he can't get it up. But the downside to this is that I end up beaten worse than normal.

Josephine takes my hand and drags me to a corner out of sight of the men, and turns me to check my back. She's a nurse and works at a free clinic over in Jackson. My shirt is lifted in the back before I realize what she's doing, only for her to gasp at the heinous sight I'm sure it is.

"Isabelle," she whispers nearly inaudibly. "You need to have these checked."

"No." I shake my head furiously. "I'm not doing anything. I'm fine. You all know I'm fine. It'll be okay. They'll heal."

"How are you standing right now?" Sutton asks, blocking anyone from seeing around her and Josephine while I shove my shirt back down.

"I'm standing because I got a text message saying one of my best friends had been in an accident, and I needed to make sure she was okay," I answer, not lying in the slightest. If it weren't for my concern for Ivy, I'd be home, in my bed.

"Everything okay?" I stiffen at the sound of the gruff but sexy tone coming from behind my friends.

Sutton whirls around and smiles as she answers. "Peachy, Angel."

Angel? That's an interesting name. It must be his road one. I've seen shows about motorcycle clubs and have read about them. I'm not completely dense.

Plus, the women I work with tell me that Hellfire Dancers is actually owned by a motorcycle club, but they rarely come in since they're not close. Mia, my boss, well the manager, she's told us all that when the owners come, she makes sure to let us all know. The woman runs a tight ship, and I think that's why I like working and driving the distance I do. Though sometimes I'll sleep in my car a couple of nights in a row to keep from exhausting myself even more with the drive home. We always get three days on, two days off.

"If that's the case, can I speak with your friend here?" Angel smirks, cocking a brow, and motions to me.

"Um, yeah," Sutton says sweetly and looks at me. "We'll be right over there."

I nod, swallowing nervously. Why does this man who I've never met want to talk to me? He's hot. Nearly as good-looking as the one with the scar on the side of his face.

Angel steps closer. His eyes seem to assess me as he clears his throat. "Didn't know one of Ivy's girls works in one of our clubs, he says, getting straight to the punch.

My eyes widen, and I visibly swallow, "Um, what?" I stammer.

"Babe," he smirks and shakes his head lowly. "Guess that's my answer. They don't know. We'll keep it between us. The only reason I know is 'cause Mia sends footage of the girls dancing every once in a while. I'm the VP of the club that owns Hellfire Dancers."

Well, shit on as stick. This isn't what I was expecting.

"You . . . um," I start.

"You don't want them to know. I get it. I'll keep it that way, but you need to tell me who the fuck hurt you."

My back stiffens at his demand.

"What?" I whisper, licking my lips nervously and wrapping my arms around my waist.

"You heard me," he states, nodding. "I'm not dumb or blind. I know the signs. You work for us, and the club takes care of its own. Your family now regardless of your employment considering who you are to Ivy."

Seriously this guy is going to give me a panic attack. "I appreciate it, but I'm okay. It's done and not going to happen again." I don't know why I'm telling him this. Maybe it's his eyes.

"Yeah, you're right. It's not going to happen again," Angel smirks. "I'll make sure of it. Keep your secrets for now, but just know I'll find out. After all, I'm deeming myself your newest best friend."

Oh my.

Ugh.

What?

"Everything good over here?"

I nearly jump out of my skin at the gruffness of the voice for the man to who that voice belongs—the guy with the scar on his face.

"Yeah, brother, I was just talking to my newest BFF." Angel chuckles and wraps an arm around my waist.

What the hell?

What alternate universe have I walked into?

The guy with the scar on his face furrows his brow at Angel, then looks down at me. His eyes are dark, assessing, and inky. And I must admit the most beautiful ones I've ever seen in my life. I could get lost looking at them, which is bad.

Very, very bad.

I can't allow it.

Nope.

My life is already hell as it is. I can't let myself be consumed by anything else.

Sitting with my friends in Reaper's room at the clubhouse, we surround Ivy. This is the first time I'm seeing her since the accident and all of us going to the hospital. I'm just thankful she's okay. We could've lost

Ivy if it weren't for the club racing after her. I swear I want to claw the eyes out of the bitch responsible for making her run away from the clubhouse right before everything went down. I'm not a violent person. I leave the violence to Josephine and Everleigh. They get off on the mess.

The girls are all talking about which guy they'd like to get it on with, and Juniper mentions how she'd love to have a chance to screw either Angel or Hellhound.

Yep, I found out his name at the hospital after Angel declared himself my best friend. I couldn't believe it. I swear it was all a joke. It had to be. Right? I'm not sure.

Angel made a point of texting me and even showing up at my apartment with food, saying he got my address from a file Mia has on me from when I applied.

I feel the way Ivy's looking at me when I don't add into the conversation, but she doesn't say anything—thank god. Instead, she changes the subject completely before we all dive back into our binge movie day.

I'm sure Ivy will try and get out of me later about what's going on, but for now, she's leaving it. I intend to make sure she doesn't get the chance to. At least not for a while. I don't even know what's happening in my own life as it is.

CHAPTER 2

HELLHOUND

Three Months Later...

After going on a run with Angel, all I want to do is go home, shower, and find some random piece to sink into for the night. I'm not even going to pick one of the P&Ps at the clubhouse. I don't use their snatches for anything other than maybe a blow job. Still, I've gotta be drunk off my ass for them to do that.

I normally prefer to go out and find a woman who hasn't been with all my brothers. Better yet, I won't have to see the bitch the next day. At the clubhouse, those women seem to think that they'll be able to lock down one of my brothers. After the stunt Claws pulled with Ivy, they all chilled marginally, but that doesn't mean they didn't keep their shit up. The P&Ps, shortened for what they really are—Pussy Pockets, seem to think we belong to them. There are a couple of them that have been trying hard to get me to fuck them, but that shit doesn't fly with me. Unless it's the mouth, I don't touch them.

Seeing the city limits for home, I relax marginally. Lately, shit's been strained, and it's only getting worse. Problems with the Triple Spirits MC are on the rise, giving us all a headache. Just this past few days, Angel and I ended up taking out a handful of the bastards who tried to sneak up on the two of us. That shit wasn't gonna fly. What I'd like to know is who gave them information in order to try to get the jump on us?

I know my VP's got the same questions rolling around in his head and will have Scythe and Styxx look into it. See what they can find for us. Scythe might be our techy guy, but when he and his brother work together as a team, they come up with a lot more shit.

Angel turns us off the main road into an apartment complex parking lot. I come to a stop next to him and park.

"What are we doing?" I ask, shutting my bike off and putting my kickstand down.

Angel smirks and shrugs. "I'm just checkin' on my BFF," he jokes, talking about Isabelle.

Fuck.

I try not to think of the damn woman. Out of all of Ivy's friends, she's the most standoffish. Sutton, Everleigh, and Josephine are all nutty but cool to talk to.

However, Juniper reminds me of the damn P&Ps, and that shit doesn't fly. I don't want that bitch in my bed, and she keeps trying to hit on me.

Reaper's made it known at the clubhouse that all Ivy's friends are off-limits unless you intend to make 'em your ol' lady—yeah, not happening. I'm not about to go there with any of them. Not that I want to anyways.

It doesn't matter to me how attractive they are all, including Isabelle.

For as standoffish as she is, Isabelle is beautiful with how shy she can be. I don't think I've ever seen another woman like her, what with her dark reddish blonde hair, freckles sprinkling along her cheeks and nose. I'll admit she's played in my mind plenty of times while I've fucked random women.

"And you couldn't do this later. Why?" I mutter, climbing off the back of my bike.

"Because I know she's off, and she's not answering my texts," he snorts, running a hand through his short hair. "So I'm gonna fuck with her. If you wanna head out, you can."

I probably should, but a part of me refuses, mostly because I want the chance to see Isabelle. Why? I don't fuckin' know other than the fact I think she's beautiful and sweet.

With a shake of my head, I follow my VP up the walkway and then the stairs to the second-story apartment. He pulls out a set of keys and unlocks the door. I didn't realize he and Isabelle were so close.

"You got a key to her place?" I quirk a brow and frown as he looks over his shoulder at me.

"Yeah, and no, it ain't fuckin' like that, brother. Isabelle and I are friends, and I look out for her," he states and pushes the door open.

"If you say so," I mutter, not liking it one bit that he's got a key though I don't have a right to even question his relationship with Isabelle.

Angel doesn't remark as he steps inside. I follow coming alert instantly at the same time he does. The living room is a total wreck.

My VP curses under his breath and pulls his gun out while slowly prowling further into the apartment and down the hallway. Standing with his back against a wall, he reaches out and pushes a door that's slightly ajar open all the way.

Immediately after, he jumps into action, shoving his gun back in his jeans and rushing to Isabelle's side. My gut tightens, and my chest burns at the sight before me as I take in all the bruises and fresh cuts along her body.

Who the fuck hurt her? Why? The sight of all the damage done to her nearly sends me spiraling back in time to when I found my sister.

Fucking hell.

"Isabelle," Angel rasps, cupping the side of her

head. "Wake up, babe." He nearly sounds heartbroken by the sight of her on the floor.

Isabelle makes a groaning noise, and her lashes flutter.

"Fuckin' hell, darlin'," Angel snaps, smoothing a strand of hair from her face. "This shit you refuse to tell me about has got to stop."

What the hell is he talking about?

"Angel?" Isabelle croaks, tears spilling from the corners of her eyes.

"Yeah," Angel grumbles. "You ready to talk to me yet?"

Isabelle groans and sits up, and her gaze widens when she sees me standing in the doorway.

"Wh-What . . . are y-you doing here?" she asks, her bottom lip trembling, and she glances between the two of us.

"Maybe you should start telling us what the fuck is going on?" I suggest not caring if my tone sounds harsh. I don't put up with drama, and if it's something that will potentially fuck with our club, then I wanna know.

"Y-you," she stutters and looks at Angel. "I can't." Tears spill faster, and she starts sobbing, shaking her head. "This doesn't have anything to do with you all, and it won't come near Ivy. I promise. Please, just leave and forget you saw me like this."

"Babe," Angel growls and helps her up to her feet

and then sits her on the edge of the bed. "Told you, no one fucks with someone who belongs to the club. You not only are Ivy's best friend, but you're also one of the best dancers at Hellfire Dancers."

Wait a fucking minute. Isabelle works for the club? Since when?

She flinches and shakes her head.

"I don't work there anymore," she whispers and drops her head, so neither of us can see her eyes.

"What do you mean?" Angel demands, tensing next to her. "Mia didn't say anything about you quitting."

"I quit today," she murmurs, shaking her head in denial. "I have another job."

I don't miss the shudder that leaves her body at the mention of this new job.

We'll see about this new job of hers.

"I think you need to explain," I snarl, not liking any of this, and I'm not going to put up with being kept in the dark. Especially after finding her beaten and bloody. Shit, I'm barely holding it together and not flipping my lid on it all.

She might not be mine or Angels, but she's his friend and Ivy's family. Meaning I'll do what I have to make sure she stays safe. I'll also do this ignoring the fact I want her for myself. However, no woman really wants a man like me.

One that's scarred as I am.

Inwardly I shake my head, pushing that thought from my mind. I go down that road, and I'll just get pissed, and I don't want that. It's in the past, and there's nothing I can do about that. What I can do is stop someone else I care for from getting hurt more than they already have been, regardless of if they want that protection or not. With Isabelle, I'm sure it'll be a fight. It's one she'll have to lose. I won't see her hurt like this again. Never a-fuckin'-gain.

CHAPTER 3

ISABELLE

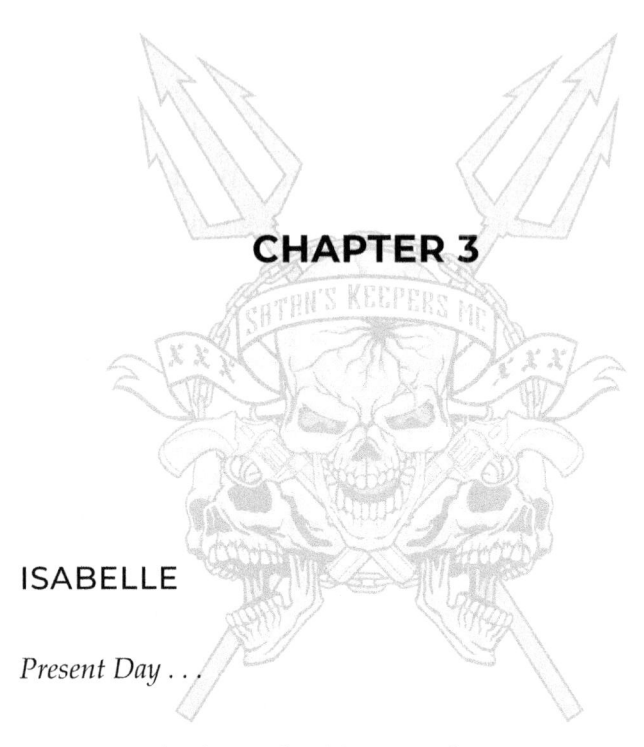

Present Day . . .

My entire body is throbbing with excruciating pain. More so, I'm complete and utterly tired of feeling helpless. That and scared out of my mind. It's been a few weeks now since things went down with Sutton and all the craziness where I ended up in the hospital.

This past year has been filled with nothing but craziness. I went from only having to hide parts of my life from my friends to keeping Angel out of my business. Then worse, Hellhound got involved a few months ago. Between both men, they've made me want to do my head in.

I mean, seriously, I don't think they've really left me

alone for more than a day. They've constantly been in my face, mostly Angel, demanding to know what I'm doing. I haven't said a word about my new job to them. I didn't want to quit working for Mia. She was cool to have as a boss, but like everything else in my life, it's never solid. Dexter found out and forced me to quit and start working at a smack house. He pretty much controls my every move.

Or he did until the other week when I'd been kidnapped and beaten worse than even Dexter has dished out in years—okay, months.

Sutton's brother or whoever the hell he was hurt me to the point I wished for death. Unfortunately, again, I'm not so lucky. I have the worst luck in the history of mankind.

Now I've got to find a way to turn my luck around at least the smallest bit. I think there's been enough drama to go around lately, and my friends and the men around here don't need more. I'm sure the moment my parents or Dexter find out where I am, they're sure to come calling, bringing it to their doorstep. I can't have that.

Why did Angel and Hellhound bring me to the clubhouse after I was discharged?

Ugh. I asked them to take me home, but of course, nope, neither listened to me.

"I need to get home," I murmur, breaking the uncomfortable silence between my friends and me while we all camp out in front of the TV with the Hallmark channel playing—not that anyone is really watching it. Well, my friends and Stella. She's a doctor who helped take care of me at the hospital. She's also Hellhound's sister. The woman told me this during my stay. "Smoky will be missing me."

I miss my cat. He's a Maine Coon and absolutely adorable. The day I got Smoky, I wasn't looking to get a pet, but one look in his pretty brown eyes, and I was hooked. He became mine, and I don't regret it. Smoky is like having a dog but in cat form. He's massive in size and demands to hog the bed. However, that order comes with him curling into me to stroke behind his ear.

"You're staying here with us," Ivy declares, her eyes coming to mine while her hand settles over her stomach protectively. "Smoky is fine. He's actually in Angel's room."

Um, what? Why didn't I know this? No one told me they took my cat from my apartment. Granted, I'm grateful he's being taken care of, but still, someone could've told me.

"I can't stay here. I don't want to be a bother." I hate being a bother. I don't like the idea of attention being directed in my direction. It always means bad things for me. I prefer to stay out of the limelight. Or, in this case, out of the way in general to keep the part of my life I've kept the girls out of away from them.

"Isabelle, you're not a bother," Sutton says, though she's not looking at me but rather past me.

I don't bother looking. I don't want to know what she's looking at. I simply need them to understand. They know what I deal with, just not all of it, to the extent it's been for years now. "You know what I mean," I whisper, meeting each of my friends' gazes as they finally let what I'm saying sink in. "I don't want them coming here, and you know they will when they find out. They'll be blitzed out of their minds—demanding money. I need to get home, get back to work, and keep them as far away as I can. I've already missed too much time . . ."

"Woman, you ain't goin' anywhere?" I jump at the snarl of Hellhound's voice right behind me, interrupting me before I can finish. I whip my head around, ignoring the pain, and find him glowering down at me. Worse, Angel's standing next to him doing the same. "You're keeping your ass right here at the clubhouse whether you like it or not."

"But . . ." I try protesting, but Angel stops me this time

"I agree," Angel growls, glancing between Hellhound and myself.

"I can't," I state, shaking my head. Neither of them knows about my folks, and I want to keep it that way.

Hellhound curls his lip in anger and leans down, narrowing his gaze, meeting mine. "You are. You're done with those fuckin' parents of yours, and that's final."

No. No. No. This can't be happening. Hellhound didn't just say that to me. Please tell me he didn't mention my parents.

Of course, he did. There's no denying it. You can see the burning anger in his eyes as he glares at me.

I'm unable to hold back the gasp. Surprised he would say that but mostly because he knows about them, period. I didn't say anything to him or Angel about my parents. The girls must have spilled something or another about my mom and dad.

I open my mouth to speak, to protest, but Hellhound shocks me once again when he reaches out and scoops me into his arms. Without thinking, I wrap my arms around his neck and hold on as he lifts me in the air, spins on his heel, and stalks down the hallway leading to where all the member's rooms are. I quickly glance over his shoulder, hoping to get help from my friends, only to find them gaping at us and Angel following hot on Hellhound's heels.

I ignore the different ranges of looks from the men who're standing around watching Hellhound carting me off. I also cringe under the death looks from the P&Ps.

My mind goes into panic mode, screaming 'Mayday' as if I am on a ship and need to jump before it sinks, taking me with it.

What do I do now?

Hellhound stops in front of a door, and Angel reaches around him and twists the knob. The door opens, and with his foot, Hellhound pushes it the rest of the way. Angel closes it behind him after we're all inside.

I find myself lowered onto an unmade bed and instantly realize we're in Hellhound's room and not Angels. I know this because the earthy masculine smell that fills it is all Hellhound.

"I want to go home," I blurt without looking at either man.

"You're not going home," Hellhound snaps harshly.

"Darlin', you ain't safe going back there."

I whip my head back and narrow my gaze on Angel at the soft tone he takes on. "What do you know? Huh? How would you know what's safe for me or not?"

Angel narrows his gaze and takes a step forward, but it's Hellhound who gets to me first.

"Bells, it doesn't take a rocket scientist to figure that shit out. But for the record, we got Scythe and Styxx to look into it. None of it we like. We've got enough going down right now with the bullshit Sutton and Ivy's egg donors are trying to pull. We don't need your shit on top of it while we're dealing. So don't fuckin' try fighting, 'cause I'll tell you now . . . you ain't gonna win."

Someone please . . . please . . . please tell me he didn't just say that?

Why am I even asking? *Of course, he said it.* This is Hellhound we're talking about. One thing I've learned in the past several months, he doesn't hold back when he has something to say. Granted, he's not much of a talker as it is, and most of the time, when he does speak up, it's harsh and mean, mainly because he's telling me what I should do.

I shake my head, blocking out the time he came with Angel to my apartment and found me on the floor. It took me pleading and begging for them not to push for answers and to keep the whole thing quiet. I pretty much threatened to run away if they said anything, though I'm sure they wanted to call me on my bluff. I have nowhere else to go, so honestly, where would I run to?

"You're staying here whether you like it or not, Bells, and those fuckin' parents of yours are nothing to you anymore. We're not about to let the shit you've been keeping to yourself slide any longer. There's more at stake here."

That's the second time Hellhound has called me Bells. What is up with that? He's always called me Isabelle. Mostly he's growled it in the past like I've been nothing more than a pain in his ass.

"Look, babe," Angel says, a little calmer. "For now, you're staying here, and that's the way it's going to stay. If you want, Smoky can stay with me while you heal, though the damn cat is going to learn to sleep on the damn floor. I'm not spooning with a furball."

I giggle softly at Angel talking about spooning Smoky.

"I want Smoky with me," I whisper, a small smile tugging on my lips.

"Not until you've healed more," Hellhound declares sternly.

"He's my cat, and I want him with me," I argue, straightening my shoulders.

"Damn thing ain't a cat, woman. He's a damn feline on steroids, and he ain't staying in this room which is where you are staying."

I swallow as Hellhound's words sink in. Staying in here? His room? Um, does that mean he's going to be in here with me?

"On that note, I see she's about to blow, and I'm out of here," Angel declares and heads for the door. He stops long enough to look back at me. "Give it a couple of days, and you'll have Smoky with you. I'm sure you'll be able to talk my brother here around into letting Smoky-boy in here."

I open my mouth to say something, but Angel is through the door, closing it behind him before I do.

A split second later, I realize I'm alone in a room with Hellhound, and I can feel his intense glare on me.

"Um . . ." I fidget nervously and pull my bottom lip between my teeth.

Hellhound watches this, and his nostrils flare in anger. Instead of speaking, he turns and stalks to his dresser, where he opens one of the top three drawers. He reaches in, pulls out a T-shirt, spins back to me, and tosses it to me. "Here. Put this on. Get some rest. I'll be back to check on you in a bit."

Without giving me a chance to speak once again, he leaves the room, slamming the door behind him.

I release a breath I didn't even realize I'd been holding and stare at the door, wondering to myself what in the world just happened. I also can't help thinking about the fact that Hellhound put me in his room and why.

CHAPTER 4

HELLHOUND

I didn't want to leave Isabelle, but if I didn't get out of my room and away from her, I don't know what I'd do. In the past months, she's gotten under my skin, and I don't know how the fuck it happened.

Wait, yeah, I do know.

The moment I saw her for the first time beaten and begging for Angel and me to just leave it be. She didn't want anyone in her business. I can understand this, but she's not a woman who should have to do anything by herself.

Fuck me. It nearly crippled me this time around when we got to Tombstone's to find she'd been hur— worse than before.

While at the hospital, Ivy, Everleigh, and Josephine opened up to Angel and me about what was going on with Isabelle. Mostly because they had to stop the nurses from calling Bells' next of kin, meaning her parents.

It was then I decided I was done fucking around. Isabelle doesn't need any more of that shit in her life, and I wasn't gonna let it continue. She's mine. She just doesn't know it yet. But she will when the time is right.

Over the past two days, I've kept a close eye on her but kept my distance. She's not left my room since I carried her ass in there. The only time I've seen her face is when I go into my room after she's fallen asleep to get my clothes. As much as I would've enjoyed curling up in bed with her, I don't. Isabelle's not ready for that shit. Soon though, I'll be there. It's just a matter of time. I want her to heal some more first.

Sighing, I turn my bike into the parking lot of the hospital without even realizing it. Earlier I left the clubhouse needing to ride my bike and get my own head right. Isabelle's closeness is fucking with my head, and I've gotta keep it clear. Now's not the time for any fuck ups. Not when two lunatic crazy bitches are out there. Because of these cunts Reaper put both Ivy, Sutton, and now Isabelle on lock down. They're not to leave the clubhouse.

I gotta give it to my Prez since he's had to put up with Ivy's anger over the fact that he won't let her go to work. She works at the garage we own and loves her job. Shit, she keeps our shit straighter than it's ever been. But regardless, he's explained to her that with her being pregnant, he won't take any chances, especially when she's getting closer to the end.

I think we'll all be happy after this pregnancy is over. Maybe then Reaper will chill a little bit. Then again, I highly doubt it. He's seriously protective over Ivy, and I can't blame him. Honestly, I understand his reasoning. I feel the same for Isabelle.

I've gotta find a way to explain this shit to her without her freaking out, but first, I gotta figure it out for myself. I know she's mine and that I intend to make that happen. What I need to wrap my head around is the fact that she's been hurt, and I didn't stop it. If I'd claimed her months ago, none of this would've happened.

Shit, a lot of things wouldn't have come to over the time since that day Angel and I found her in her apartment.

Inwardly shaking my head, I park and stare up at the hospital. Why did I come here? It's not like I need to go in there.

I know the reason, Stella. She's inside working. Since Ivy's accident, my sister has been coming around more, but neither of us has spoken to each other. It's not easy to be near her. Mostly because I feel like a failure. I fucked up with her. Instead of being reasonable, I sent her ass packing, straight to Ireland, where she stayed for a while before moving back. I've always kept tabs on Stella, mostly through our Uncle Luke Ryan or his son, our cousin, Connor.

Only my brothers know about the blood relations I have with my father's family, and because of that, we have an alliance with the Black Clovers, who work closely with the Ryan family. However, our club stays out of their business, and they give us the same courtesy, but they're there for us if we need them. The same goes the other way around as well.

Thinking about Connor, I smirk, remembering the last summer I was in Ireland. It was before the accident that took Stella's and my parents from us. I nearly lost Stella that night as well. Maybe that's why I flipped on her in such a harsh way because she'd not listened and put herself in danger.

Shit.

I release a breath of frustration and shake my head, my gaze going to the doors. I know my sister goes in and out almost daily. She lives and breathes this place. I realized this after overhearing Ivy and her talking about it not long ago.

I should probably talk to her, but how the fuck do I do that. It's not like she's speaking to me either. Our relationship as siblings is fucked.

Leaning forward, I brace my forearms on the handles of my bike, my brows creasing in the middle of my forehead.

I briefly close my eyes and look up to the sky. If our

parents were still alive, they'd be beyond pissed that Stella and I aren't close. That I didn't look out for her as I should have. A pain in my chest tightens, and I'm left feeling the way I always do—nothing but agony. I sacrificed a lot when I lost my parents and then my family. I turned my back on Stella. Now I'm suffering the consequences.

Which leaves me wondering how I can make sure Isabelle understands what she means to me. But more than that, how do I get past the pain of everything?

"Fuck," I growl, sitting back up and gripping the handles of my bike. I kickstart my girl and, with one last look to the doors leading into the hospital, I hit the throttle and leave, heading for the clubhouse. It's time I talk to Isabelle and get some things straight between the two of us.

The moment I get to the clubhouse, I know without a doubt something's not right. I just can't put my finger on it. I step into the main room of the clubhouse and scan the room. I spot Smoky lying on the couch next to Angel. Damn cat seems to have taken over the place.

Shit, I wouldn't even call Smoky a cat. He's bigger than a Jack Russel, just fluffier. Smoky, however, does seem to fit in with his always grouchy expression. The damn animal reminds me of one of those cats they always have those memes about.

Angel glances in my direction and gives me a chin lift. "Where you been?" he asks, turning his attention back to the game on TV ... Longhorns vs. Jayhawks.

"Out ridin'." I shrug, crossing my arms over my chest. "Why?"

"No reason."

Yeah, right. No reason, my ass. With my Prez and VP, there's always something. Neither of them mentions anything without there being a reason.

Deciding to leave it for the time being, I drop my arms and head for the hallway leading to my room. I ignore the others calling out to me. Especially the damn P&Ps. They know I don't want them, and yet they still try.

At my door, I take a second to breathe and turn the knob. Soon as I push the door open, I realize what the fuck feeling of something not being right is.

"Isabelle," I call out, already knowing she's nowhere in the room or in the bathroom—the light was off, and the door was open.

Motherfucker.

Spinning on my heel, I storm back down the hall, my gaze locking on my VP, who's doing the same by staring at me. "Where the fuck is she?"

"Tried to stop her, but she wasn't having it. You know I can't stand tears, especially when it's hers," he mutters, slouching deeper into the corner of the couch. "Bells became my little sister, and you know what that means when I say it." Yeah, I did know. "I let her go home, but only because I've got a prospect on her and knew as soon as you found out, you'd lose your shit."

He's not wrong about that.

Narrowing my gaze, I clench my jaw and ball my hands into fists at my sides.

"You gonna go get her back?" Angel asks, cocking a brow.

"You fuckin' know I am," I snap, curling my lip in anger.

"Good, that means you claimin' her?"

"Yeah, it means I'm fuckin' claimin' Bells. She's fuckin' mine." On that, I stalk toward the doors and out to my bike. It's gonna take all my self-control to keep my anger at bay when I get my hands on Isabelle. She knew she wasn't supposed to leave the clubhouse, yet she used tears on Angel to get her way and that shit ain't gonna fly with me.

CHAPTER 5

ISABELLE

Laying on my couch, I curl into a ball letting the tears spill down my cheeks. I don't know what came over me in the past two days, but I can't help crying. It all comes down to the fact that my life is spiraling out of control.

Two days I spent at the clubhouse feeling a sense of vulnerability because of Hellhound. I don't understand why but being in his room had me thinking craziness. My life is already a mess of lunacy because of all the shit going down in it—add in what happened recently, it's become more so.

When Hellhound left me in his room, he didn't come back like he said he would. Well, I don't think he did. Though it's his room, he could've come in there while I'd been asleep and didn't wake me. I know he didn't get in the bed next to me, however.

Ugh, shit, tears roll down my cheeks thinking about Hellhound. In the past months, he's come around me more and more but kept his distance at the same time. Now I'm confused all over again. Mainly because he put me in his room and then left. I want to think something of it. I do, only I heard the P&Ps talking this morning when I went to get a cup of coffee from the kitchen.

I squeeze my eyes shut, remembering it.

"I cannot believe, Hellhound is letting that skanky bitch stay in his room," Chops says, stopping me from entering the kitchen. She's one of the girls that Ivy explained to me a while back as one of the P&Ps, otherwise known as Pussy Pockets. Evidently, that's what the members of the club call the clubwhores—women who want to do nothing but fuck the brothers and party.

"You can't believe it. Oh please, I was starting to think he was gay since he refused me," another one of the women, I think her names Poppers, snaps. "I mean, I offer him something, and he throws me to the side."

"At least I've gotten to have his cock."

I shudder thinking about that. I didn't wait around to hear the rest because I turned on my heels and rushed away from there, and hid in Hellhound's room. It took a lot out of me to do it, but I begged and pleaded with Angel to let me come home. He didn't want to at first. In the end, he gave in to me when I started crying, saying I needed to be in my space.

He brought me home and left but only after declaring Smoky was staying at the clubhouse. I started to argue. Only he wouldn't listen. This is because I know he digs my cat. Smoky has all but made himself at home at the clubhouse, and I didn't have the heart to take him away from there just yet. I'll bring him home soon after I figure out what I'm going to do next.

Maybe I should run away—take what money I do have still and rush off on a plane. I could go to Mexico and find a job in a cantina or, better yet, fly to Florida and get a job as a bartender. They get a lot of tourists throughout the year. I'd never be low on tips.

Someone knocks on the door intruding on my thoughts, and pulls me out of my head. I press a hand into the couch and shove against the cushion to sit up, my eyes on the door. It could be a number of people on the other side of it, and none of them is anyone I want to see right now. Especially Hellhound.

Standing, I reach up and run my fingers through my loose hair while I look down at my clothes, making sure I look okay. Dressed in a pair of yoga leggings with a bright purple band at my waist, I paired it with a grey tank top. I don't have to look at my hair to know it's a mess—it's always a mess, in my opinion.

Sometimes I wonder if I'm even related to my parents because of the fact that I don't look anything like them. Where I have dark reddish blonde hair, they have brown. My eyes are bluish-green, and theirs are hazel. The only reason I know I'm related to them is the fact that my mom's blood type is the same as mine. Granted, it's not a DNA test. I like to think of that as something. Of course, I could be an idiot to think that.

I shake my head, not even worrying about going down that train of thought, and rush for the door sucking in a breath in preparation. I barely get the door unlocked before it's shoved open, and Dexter comes barging in.

My heart leaps in fear at the sight of him. "Dex-Dexter, wh-what are y-you doing h-here?" I stutter, staring up at him with wide eyes as I back away from him.

Dexter slams the door shut, that malicious grin of his securely in place. "Where you been, Isa?" The simple question comes out in mocking concern from his deep baritone voice. With one look in his eyes, I know he's not drunk or high. "Ain't seen you in weeks now, baby. You had me concerned. Thought I was gonna have to whack your folks for the debt they owe."

I swallow nervously and back up further, hitting the wall behind me right next to the hallway leading to my room. "I-I was in the hospital," I say fearfully.

"Yeah?" Dexter smirks, closing in on me. "Doesn't change shit between you and me. I fuckin' own you, and yet you seem to think you can do whatever the fuck you want. Go where you want. Fuck who you want. Hide from me. You also fuckin' know the consequences of not doing what you're told."

Before I know it, Dexter's hand is wrapping around my throat and squeezing tightly. My lips part, trying to breathe through my mouth, but he's cutting all air off. Tears well in my eyes as I pry at his hand, trying to get him to let me go.

"You gotten in with that fuckin' club in town . . . decided to become a whore for them. Give them that body that belongs to me, huh?" Dexter spits, narrowing his gaze and cocking his head marginally to the side.

I know whenever he does this to brace for something more—something horrible.

Why can't my life be simple?

All I've ever wanted was to simply be left alone in peace.

My vision blurs, and I become lightheaded. I fear he'll finally kill me as I've prayed for several times since the first time he raped me years ago. However, that's not the case. Instead, Dexter steps back and uses his hand at my throat to sling me to the floor.

I roll to my side and curl into a ball, anticipating

what's next to come. I suck in a breath and cough, trying to catch my breath. My throat is throbbing, and I'm sure the bruises that were fading from what Sutton's stepbrother left on me are now going to be replaced with worse ones. It takes everything in me to keep from crying as Dexter flips me onto my back and straddles me.

"You're gonna learn, Isabelle, and you're gonna do it once and for all. You fuckin' belong to me bitch, and I'm not letting you get away with giving others what belongs to me," he snarls, pulling his fist back, ready to punch me.

I brace myself for the hit, but it never comes.

"What the fuck?" Dexter yells. "Who the fuck do you think you are?"

I breathe a sigh of relief, but it's only for a brief moment as I realize what is happening. Through blurry eyes, I try to focus on the fact that Hellhound is standing with his hand around Dexter's throat, holding his hand

Oh my God! What is Hellhound doing here? Why did he come here?

Hellhound makes a gruff growling sound and slams Dexter hard against the wall. "Doesn't matter who the fuck I am," he snarls.

I scamper to my feet, keeping my gaze locked on Hellhound. From just the side view of him, he scares the hell out of me. The fury rolling off him is suffocating at best. This is the man who earned his name in the club, not the one I've seen on the occasions, which can be nice. Granted, he's the same person regardless. Just right now, he's pissed.

"Let go of me," Dexter gasps, fighting against Hellhound's hold, but he's not doing a good job of escaping. Hellhound isn't budging.

Bonus for Hellhound, he's also got a good amount of weight over Dexter. I'm sure it's all muscle too.

"Hellhound," I croak, clearing my throat and wincing. He whips his head in my direction, shooting me a look with anger filling his gaze. Hellhound looks me over for a split second and turns his focus back to Dexter.

"Come near her again, and you'll get a bullet between your eyes." Without waiting for a response, Hellhound moves, dragging Dexter to the door, and throws him out into the breezeway before slamming the door.

From the way his chest is rising and falling, I wait nervously, not sure if I should say anything.

Hellhound doesn't look at me, nor does he speak. Instead, he shoves a hand in his pocket and pulls his phone out. He swipes his finger along the screen before lifting it up to his ear. A few seconds later, he finally opens his mouth as he slowly brings his gaze to mine. "Tombstone, send a few brothers over to Isabelle's apartment. She's officially moving out of this shithole and into the clubhouse."

Um, what?

My eyes widen, and I watch Hellhound closely as he waits for a second more and grunts something incoherent, then pulls the phone away from his ear. He slides it back in his pocket and stalks in my direction.

I open my mouth to say something, but Hellhound doesn't give me the chance to speak. He curls an arm around me, the other he uses to reach up and tangle his fingers in my hair as he brings his lips down on mine.

I part my lips on a gasp, and Hellhound takes the opening to thrust his tongue in, claiming me while pulling me closer. I close my eyes and clutch at his shirt. Hellhound ends the kiss just as quickly as he started it.

My eyes flutter open to find his gaze locked on me, examining me as I get my bearings.

When I do, he shocks me again when he tightens his hand in my hair, holding my attention so I don't try and pull away.

"You fucked up Bells, and it's time we fuckin' talk about this bullshit, but first, you pack your shit." The way his eyes flare and nostrils seem to fume, I wonder if, at any moment if he'll breathe fire.

As much as I'd like nothing more than to say something to him, I realize it's not the time for it. But I reserve the right to go off on him later after we get back to the clubhouse. Hellhound did just keep me from being hurt once again, though that doesn't mean I'm going to let him off the hook for making decisions for me. No matter how grateful I am for him saving me this time around.

CHAPTER 6

HELLHOUND

It takes all of my control not to go off on Isabelle for leaving the safety of the clubhouse. If she hadn't left, this shit wouldn't have happened. She wouldn't have new bruises forming on her throat.

Fucking bullshit is what this is. I'm not just pissed at her, though. The damn prospect didn't protect her like he should have. Fucker knew the moment he stepped into the apartment, he fucked up. His face paled as he started to apologize.

I didn't want to hear it, and he knew it. Ghoul is a good prospect for the most part, he and Goblin both. The fact he knows he fucked up means he'll step up and make sure shit doesn't happen again.

Within two hours, we've got all of Isabelle's shit

packed up and out of the apartment. I haven't said another word to her, and she kept silent throughout the entire event. Though I made sure she was in reaching distance, and my eyes stayed on her—not letting her out of my sight. I'm still pissed over her leaving the clubhouse. More than that, I'm furious over what that motherfucker was trying to do, whatever the fuck it is he was going to do. I wanted to kill him. I would've if it weren't for my woman being in the room. I saw the fear in her eyes and didn't want to scare her further than she already was.

Now that we've got everything loaded, it's time to put her ass on the back of my bike and get back to the clubhouse. I had Angel text my sister and ask her to come check on Bells after she got off work. I don't think the bastard did any damage, but you never know for sure.

Once my brothers leave the apartment, I take Isabelle's hand and pull her with me to the door. "You're on the bike with me," I declare, not looking back at her. I'm afraid if I do, I'll kiss her again, and that shit ain't happening, not now when I've got to get her to safety.

Kissing Isabelle earlier was a mistake but one I don't regret. The next time I've got my mouth on hers, I want it to be in my room at the clubhouse where I can give her the attention she deserves. It also needs to be after I make sure she's not hurt and I've got full control over my anger.

At my bike, I look at Isabelle and put my helmet on her head.

"I've never been on a bike," she whispers, eyes wide, and licks her bottom lip.

My dick twitches behind its confines, liking the innocence.

"Then get ready for your first of many, *Críona*." I grin. My chest constricts, knowing I'll be the only one she rides with.

Swinging a leg over, I straddle my bike and motion for Isabelle to do the same. She mimics my actions and climbs on behind me. Isabelle places her hands tentatively on my waist, but I grab her wrists and pull them firmly around me. By doing this, I also bring her front flush with my back. After getting her positioned the way I want her, I kick up the stand and start my bike. Isabelle makes a squeal and tightens her grip around me, holding me tighter.

I take the long way back to the clubhouse, enjoying having her with me, giving her this new adventure. She's never experienced something as freeing or, well, not like this. I know she and her friends ride four-wheelers whenever they get the chance. Granted, as far as I know, it's been a while since Ivy, Sutton, and Isabelle have been out riding.

I finally pull into the clubhouse parking area, back in between Angel and Tombstone's bikes, kick down the stand, and motion for Isabelle to hop off. I swing my leg over and climb off behind her. Taking her hand in one of mine, I bring her closer and use my free hand to remove the helmet from her head and hang it on the handlebars.

"Come on," I mutter, tugging her hand, pulling her behind me. I don't stop when I all but drag her into the clubhouse or for anyone who looks like they want to ask what's going on. Isabelle was smart enough not to fight me or, better yet, speak up. I don't want to do this shit in front of my brothers or anyone else. This shit is between the two of us, and that's it.

The moment we're behind closed doors of my room, I let go of Isabelle's hand and spin on her, planting my hands on my hips. "What the fuck is in your head leaving the clubhouse in the first fuckin' place?"

Isabelle blinks up at me and takes a step backward, her hands fidgeting with the hem of her top.

"Not got an answer?" I snarl harshly.

"What do you want me to say?" she whispers, diverting her gaze from mine. "I wanted to go home. It's not like you care. I mean, why did you even put me in here in the first place. Or come to the apartment when you found out I wasn't here?"

Shaking my head, I close the distance between the

two of us and grip either side of her waist. "You think I didn't want you here?"

"It's pretty obvious."

"How's that?" I demand, already knowing the answer because I've been fucking avoiding her the past few days since putting her in here.

Isabelle brings her gaze to mine and narrows those beautiful eyes on me. Straightening her shoulders, she answers, "It doesn't matter. Just get out of my way, and I'll go find Ivy or Sutton. They can show me where I can stay. Or I'll stay with Angel."

"The fuck you will." I curl my lip at the mere thought of Isabelle with anyone else but me. "You aren't staying anywhere else but right here in this room with me."

"Why?" Isabelle tenses and shakes her head. "You don't like me and can barely stand to be in the same room with me. Sure, you've been around me over the past months, making excuses as to being around me, but still, you don't know me, and you can't stand the sight of me for more than a few minutes. Especially since what happened with Sutton's stepbrother." She screams the last part, tears spilling down her cheeks as if she's in pain.

I yank her flush against my front and reach up to tangle my fingers of one hand in her hair, holding her head back, so she's looking at me. "I don't fuckin' hate you. It's the opposite. I stayed away so I wouldn't do anything you're not ready for. But that all ends now. *You're mine*, Isabelle, *and* you're gonna learn quick, I'm not putting up with this bullshit. You not listening to me. Today you earned yourself a spanking for the stunt you pulled."

"You are not gonna spank me," she gasps, trying to shove against my chest.

"By my count, *Críona*, your leaving the safety of the clubhouse earned you five, then that shit at the apartment earned you another five. But Imma wait 'til you're not hurt to give 'em to you."

"Hellhound, you are not spanking me, and you are not going to do anything to me," she snaps. "I'm also not anything to you."

"Now that just bought you three more, bringing your total to thirteen. Keep racking them up, baby. I don't mind." I smirk, lowering my head to touch my forehead to hers. "Also, from now on, when we're in here or anywhere alone, you don't call me Hellhound. I'm not Hellhound to you."

"And what am I supposed to call you?" she demands, her voice taking on a snarky tone I've never heard before from her. It goes straight to my dick that's already hard for her.

I smirk and hold her tighter and lower my lips and brush them against hers as I answer, "Asher." Without giving her a chance to retort, I claim her mouth the way I wanted, thrusting my tongue in to mingle with hers.

After the initial shock of my kissing her, Isabelle relaxes into me, allowing me to deepen our kiss further. I take the opportunity and decide my next plan of attack when it comes to my woman and showing her she's mine.

CHAPTER 7

ISABELLE

Asher.

Hellhound's name is Asher, and he's kissing me.

Not just kissing me but *kissing* me. My body reacts in a way it's never reacted before—coming alive at his touch, at the closeness between the two of us.

Without realizing what I'm doing, I slide my hands up his chest and wrap them around his neck. I lift up on my tiptoes and press deeper into his body. Hellhound takes this movement in stride, releases my hair and waist to cup my ass, and lifts me up off my feet, so I have no choice but to wrap my legs around his waist.

Hellhound groans an approval against my mouth and moves deeper into the room until he's lowering me onto the bed. Everything seems to spiral out of control from there. Shirts are yanked off—my doing.

Hellhound takes his time removing my shirt and bra. He uses his mouth along my skin, not leaving an inch of me untouched as he lowers himself until he's face to face with my breasts. His eyes lift to meet mine as I watch him through lust-filled eyes. I draw my lower lip between my teeth at what I see in his heated ones. It's a look I've never seen before.

If I'm honest, this is the first time anything like this has happened that I'm not repulsed and wishing to end it all.

Hellhound flicks his tongue against a hardened nipple and pinches the other. Rotating between the two, he gives both my breast his undivided attention. My body is humming with the need for more. More of him doing just that and other things.

Kissing his way further down my stomach, Hellhound leaves my breasts and uses both hands to grip either side of my waistband. He yanks my leggings down in one swift motion, removing them altogether.

"Hellhound," I gasp, earning a heated look from him.

"Told you, Bells, you don't call me that," he says, hooking my legs in his arms and spreading them enough for him to settle between them. Hellhound leans in and blows out a breath of air against my entrance.

"Asher," I moan, arching my back.

"Like that, *Críona*?"

I bite my lower lip and nod in answer.

Taking that as my response, Hellhound dives in, taking his time slowly driving me insane with his touch. Fingers. Mouth. All of it. Something I've never felt before starts to take over, and I thrash against the bed.

"Asher, something . . ."

"Ride it out, *Críona*, come for me," he orders and flicks his tongue against my clit.

I do as he commands and arch my back as my release takes over and cry out his name.

Breathing heavily, I watch him through little slits as he comes over me and rolls to his side, and pulls me into his arms. Tilting his head down, Hellhound captures my lips in a breathy kiss. His hands roam over my exposed skin, sending shivers of pleasure throughout my entire being.

"Fuckin' like how you come alive for me," he murmurs, his mouth brushing mine with each word. "Can't wait to see what you're like when I'm actually inside you."

I blush and draw my bottom lip between my teeth.

"How's that throat?" he asks, brushing a finger lightly along the curve where my neck and shoulder meet.

I clear my throat and answer him. "It hurts, but it's nothing I can't handle."

Hellhound's eyes flash with anger, but he quickly

hides it and nods. "Come on, let's get you dressed and checked out. Stella is probably already here."

My brows draw in, and I do something stupid. "Why don't you talk to your sister?" I blurt out the question.

Hellhound shakes his head and gets up, pulling me with him. "When you trust me with your story, I'll give you mine. Until then, I'm not answering that question."

Oh, boy, was that an answer of all answers. Me tell him all that is me to get all of him or not find out the truth behind him and Stella. Whatever it is has to be big. But do I really want him to know the ugliness of my past? Can I trust him to understand? What happens when he finds out and thinks I'm as hideous as my parents are? I've struggled my entire life trying to have a small margin of peace I get with my friends around me. With him around, it could be stripped from me quicker than ripping a band-aid off a wound.

I squeeze my eyes shut and inwardly shake my head at my own thoughts. The what if's and maybe questions aren't going to get me anywhere. Sutton and Ivy have both proven this to be not the case. They both have men now—men who adore them and would do anything for them. I've seen it firsthand with both Reaper and Tombstone, but I don't think I could handle a man sacrificing himself to my level and bringing me back to where I want nothing more than to be.

I give Hellhound a nod as I redress myself back in my leggings and tank top while under the direct gaze of Hellhound. I meet his gaze briefly before he moves, rounding me and to his closet. He opens the door and pulls out a flannel long-sleeve button-up.

"Put this on over your tank, *Críona*."

Without questioning him, I take the shirt and put it on over my arms, savoring the warmth of the thick material as well as the smell of him surrounding me. Not just the room, either. I hold his gaze while doing up a couple of buttons in the middle.

Hellhound takes my hand and pulls me close. "I don't know what was going through your head just now, but know this, *Críona*, you're my woman. I'm not about to let any more shit happen to you. Not if I can help it."

Again, I nod, only this time, tears threaten to spill down my cheeks. No one, and I mean no one, knows the depths of my struggles, yet here Hellhound is declaring I'm no longer alone. I'm not sure if I should run as far away as I can or burrow into him and hold on tight.

CHAPTER 8

HELLHOUND

"Try not to get hurt anymore," Stella says, stepping away from Isabelle after giving her a once over. "Rest and drink liquids as much as you can."

"Okay," Isabelle murmurs, nodding. "Thank you for coming to check to make sure I'm okay."

I glance from Isabelle to my sister to find her avoiding me as I've done her.

"No problem, I've got to go home and get ready for my date now," Stella answers, packing her medical bag.

"Date?" Sutton questions, quirking a brow. "With who? You didn't tell us you were seeing someone?"

I don't want to hear this conversation, but at the same time, I'm not leaving Isabelle's side. Not for anything.

Stella quickly looks at me and then back to Sutton. "I, um, I . . . just a guy I've met through a friend."

"What's he look like?" Ivy asks, sitting close but distant enough, so no one bumps into her round stomach. She and Reaper are due to have their baby any day now. No one knows what they're having as they'd opted not to find out. Mainly because Ivy's still freaked out about becoming a parent, but what she's gotta get into her head is she's not alone, and she's not gonna screw up being a mom. Reaper ain't gonna allow her to, and neither will any of us. We've all got her back.

Glancing over to my Prez, I smirk, seeing the way he's glowering at Ivy. "What the fuck do you need to know what he looks like?"

Ivy leans to the side of her chair and tilts her head back to look at Reaper. "Don't take that tone with me, mister. It's not like I'm not carrying your child in me. I simply want to know for future reference in case we girls have to send someone out to beat anyone up."

At this, Sutton outright laughs, and Isabelle giggles softly.

The sound of her voice draws my attention as she tilts her face upward to meet my gaze. My dick twitches at the blush crossing her cheeks.

Fucking hell.

I wanna know what's on her mind. I hope it's about me being between her legs, my mouth on her pussy. I couldn't hold back from getting a taste of her but I wasn't gonna fuck her. Not yet. I needed to know she wasn't hurt worse by that motherfucker.

Which reminds me, I gotta speak with my brothers. Not just about the reason behind Isabelle's freshly bruised neck, but the whole fuckin' situation. It's time they all know just how deep the shit she's been in. They've also gotta know, all of 'em, that Isabelle's my woman, and I'm not putting up with the bullshit this motherfucker could try and pull.

I know the fucker's a dealer and he's gonna try something thinking he's got weight in our town. Unfortunately for him, he doesn't get shit. This area is our territory.

I ignore the girl's conversation and lean down, pressing my forehead to Isabelle's. "Don't go outside or try to leave the clubhouse. I gotta meet with my brothers, then you and I will order a pizza or something. Got me?"

Isabelle nods in response, pulling away slightly.

I straighten and reach out to stroke her cheek gently. Isabelle parts her lips, and the blush on her cheeks deepens.

Moving away from her, I catch my brothers' eyes locked on me. With a shake of my head, I head for the room we hold church and wait for the rest of them to join in. Reaper's the last one to step into the room before closing the door behind him.

"Right, what the fucks going on?" he demands,

taking his place at the head of the table. His eyes locked on me.

"Went to Isabelle's apartment to drag her back to the clubhouse. Didn't care if I had to do it kicking and screaming," I start and look at Angel. "She shouldn't have left in the first place."

"Brother, you have a woman in tears telling you all she wants to do is go home, then you talk to me about that shit," Angel mutters, narrowing his gaze. "But you're right. She shouldn't have gone home. Now what the fuck happened?"

"What happened is, is I walked into her apartment to find the motherfucker she refused to tell us about nearly strangling her to death," I answer, my lip curling. "Fucker was on top of her, hands around her throat."

"Fuck," Angel snarls, slams his fist on the table, and leans back in his chair.

"You can say that again," I growl and glance around the table.

"One of you wanna explain to the class what we don't know but seems you both do?" Reaper's harsh tone vibrates throughout the room.

I glance around the table and rap my knuckles while meeting each of my brothers' hard gazes. "Isabelle refuses to tell us what's going on . . . but I know the guy who beat her is her parents' dealer."

"Isabelle, your woman?" Scythe asks calmly, but

there's something in his gaze that doesn't sit right. He's sitting forward and bracing his elbows on the table, hands clasped together.

I take in his face briefly, trying to figure out where he's going with this, and nod. "Yeah, she's mine."

"Then I'll tell you I've looked into her. I've done this with each and every one of those women," he retorts and looks from me to Tombstone, then Reaper. "No fuckin' way am I gonna let anymore shit come down on either Sutton or Ivy. So in order to do that, I dug into each of the women's backgrounds, and I know more about them than they'll ever want me to know."

"What do you know?" Angel's tone changes to one that we all know is deadly.

"Isabelle pays her parents' drug debt."

Shit.

"You shitting me?" Reaper sneers curling his lip. "Who the fuck makes their kid pay for them to be high?"

"Prez, far as I know, Isabelle's been paying that particular bill since she was a teenager. There's a report of her being at the hospital at sixteen. She claimed to have been in an accident, but notes in the report say she showed signs of being raped."

My fury grows the more Scythe tells us. It's all I can do to keep my shit together and continue to listen.

"From all accounts, it looks as if she not only went

to school but worked two jobs from the age of fourteen until recently when she started working at Hellfire Dancers."

"Wait, she was one of our dancers?" Daemon interrupts.

"Yeah, she worked there," Angel confirms for Scythe. "Mia said she'd been one of the best dancers we had. I've got a video she sent me when Isabelle first started." Angel brings his gaze to mine and smirks. "Don't worry. It was before you entered the picture, and she's still got clothes on. One thing about Isabelle going on stage, she never took her top off. According to Mia, the customers like that about her. End of each dance, she'd turn her back to the crowd, untie the top, and the lights on her darkened."

"Better fuckin' delete that shit, but send it to me first," I grumble, not liking the fact he's got a video of Isabelle, and I've never seen her dance.

"Right," Angel smirks.

"Anyways, what you all should know is Dexter, the dealer Hellhound is talking about, has put the word out she's his property. He's the reason she was forced to quit working at our club. He forced her to do other things for him in his establishments, though I wouldn't call them businesses." Scythe shakes his head before his gaze locks on mine. "You should know Isabelle's parents don't give a shit about her, never have. But I'm sure they'll come calling. She's the reason they're still alive."

"What I want to know is why she's paid for their habits?" Tombstone mutters.

"Better yet, why didn't she escape them years ago?" Ghost grunts.

"Right, so, here's the kicker in this story, brothers. Isabelle isn't her parents' daughter," Scythe says nonchalantly, dropping the information like it were a bomb ready to go off at any time.

"Come again?" I demand, brows creasing in the middle of my forehead. "What do you mean they aren't her parents?"

"What I mean is, when they took her blood at the hospital, I asked Stella for a sample. Had my cousin, Finnegan, run a DNA test."

"You went to Finnegan?" Styxx demands, slamming his hand open palm to the table. "What the fuck?"

We all knew who Finnegan was and what he does for a living. He's one of the best out there in what he does. Him and the organization he runs. They're not men to mess with. It's him and his men who taught Scythe to do what he does. Same with Styxx. That doesn't mean my brothers are cool with their cousin.

"Yeah, I did cause shit wasn't adding up," Scythe defends himself. "And I was fuckin' right. Isabelle was kidnapped when she was fifteen months old. Her real name is Isabelle Hayes."

"What the fuck?" Styxx explodes, coming out of his seat. "You tellin' me that . . ." he points his finger to the door, "sh-she's our . . ."

"Yeah, brother," Scythe says coolly, coming out of his own chair. "She's our little sister. Our baby sister."

"Fuck," Styxx roars. He grips either side of his head, tilts his head back, and bellows as he collapses to his knees. The pain radiating off him hits all of us in the gut.

Scythe moves as we all do, but he gets to his twin brother's side first and starts talking to him soft enough that no one can hear what he's saying.

My world feels as if it's spinning on its axis at this revelation. We all know Scythe and Styxx story. It's not a pretty one. The night their parents were brutally killed, they also lost their sister. No one could find her body, though it was assumed she was dead. Now come to find out, she's been in our town this entire time.

Fuck. I feel for my brothers.

I look from Scythe and Styxx to Angel, then back to the twins. They lost their sister years ago and thought they'd never see her again. Now they have her, and she doesn't even know any of this shit. Isabelle's world is about to be rocked more than it already has.

Shit.

I don't even want to think about what this could do to her.

Staring into the dark sky, I watch the stars shimmering. After Scythe's revelation about Isabelle, Reaper dismissed everyone for the time being. Styxx left with Scythe, Beast, Ghost, and Daemon following him.

I don't know what's going through his head, but I'm sure they'll get him straightened out. We all will.

I blow out a puff of smoke from the joint I lite up and lean against the side of the clubhouse. Isabelle's sound asleep in my bed, and I needed to be out here. To figure out my own head.

My phone rings in my pocket, keeping me from going deep down the dark road. I pull it out to find it's Sledge calling me. He's the Prez of the Black Clover MC. Curious as to what he's calling me for, I answer. "Yeah?"

"Got a message for you to call Connor," he says gruffly and hangs up, not waiting for my response.

Fuck me, whatever it is, it has gotta be urgent. Normally Sledge doesn't hang up.

I find Connor's phone number and hit the send icon on the screen. Connor answers on the third ring. "I see Sledge didn't waste time in getting you my message." He chuckles.

"What, you couldn't call me yourself?" I snort and lift the joint to my lips.

"I could've, but this was more fun," he laughs, and I can imagine the shit-eating grin he's got on his face.

"Right, what did you need, Con? I know this isn't gonna be a social call. Not if you want me calling this time of night."

"Reason I'm calling is the fact Stella's got a marriage contract, and if we don't get her back here and married to him soon, we're looking at an alliance being broken."

I clench my teeth and pinch the bridge of my nose. I can't catch a fucking break. Blowing out a breath, I stare into the shadows. "You expect me to send her back to Ireland and make her go through with a marriage contract?"

"Asher, you know this is what happens in our families," Connor says, calm yet stern.

"Yeah, I fuckin' know. But I *also* know I'm not sending my fuckin' sister to marry a man who I sure as fuck *don't* know. I'm *definitely* not gonna let my sister go through any more pain than she already has. You know what happened before I sent her ass there fifteen years ago. You think I'll put her through more? What if it were you in my shoes and it was *your* sister?"

Connor's silent for a moment, most likely thinking about what I've said. He's as protective of his sister as I am of Stella. It doesn't matter if I talk to her or not. I'm not gonna let anything happen to her. Not now. Not ever again.

"I'll look into seeing if there's another way around it. If I can't, we're looking at war, Asher, but I get you, and I'll do what I can for Stella," Connor says quietly.

"Appreciate it," I mutter and finish the conversation with him, telling me he'll check in soon.

Pulling the phone from my ear, I stand and shove the damn thing in my pocket and put out my joint. With a heavy breath, I head back into the clubhouse and to my room. I strip out of my clothes and climb into bed, wrap my arms around Isabelle, and breathe in her flowery scent. I instantly calm and relax in a way the joint didn't help.

I close my eyes and allow sleep to claim me, at least for a couple of hours.

CHAPTER 9

SCYTHE

I knew when Styxx found out what I figured out months ago, he'd lose it. Following him now to the cemetery where our parents are buried, I have a sickening feeling in the pit of my stomach. Whatever's going through my brother's head isn't good. I jerk a chin to our brothers, who follow, telling them to hold back. Styxx already broke once. He doesn't need them to witness it again.

Years ago, our parents were killed in a home invasion. Our little sister was only fifteen months old at the time and barely walking. She had a cold that day, and Mom and Dad stayed home with her while we went to a birthday party for our cousin Finnegan. We got home to find our mom's throat slashed, her body brutally beaten. Dad took a bullet to the back of the head after also taking a beating. We both freaked and went looking for Isabelle. There was blood everywhere, but no body.

For a while, they looked for her. There was an Amber alert and everything. No signs of her being found.

The first time I saw her at the hospital after Ivy's wreck, something about her seemed familiar to me. At the time, I let it be. The longer she was around, though, the more I started thinking. It was when we were at our aunt and uncles a few weeks before what went down with Sutton. They raised us like their own sons. We're still tight with them and go for dinners all the time, considering our aunt will have a hemorrhage if we're not there. While at their house, I saw a picture that I've seen thousands of times before, but this time it dawned on me why I felt the way I did about Isabelle. She looks like our mom.

I didn't know what to do at the time. I wanted to confide in someone, but I didn't. I kept it to myself. If I was wrong, I wasn't taking the chance of getting anyone's hopes up. It was all on me.

With what went down at Tombstone's with Sutton and seeing how Isabelle was injured, I took the chance to find the truth without approach. I got the blood sample, took it to Finnegan, and had him run for the results. He didn't ask questions, not until after. My cousin has his own organization, one that even freaks me out with the jobs they do. Guess you can say he's like GI Joe without the military backing him. He's a private contractor with his own men taking his back.

After getting the results, I sat on the information and dug deep into Isabelle's past. I also watched as my brother, Hellhound, staked his claim on her. I didn't know how I felt about it at first, but then again, I didn't grow up with my sister, and she's a complete stranger no matter if I held her as a baby in my arms when I was five. Now the information has been shared, and I've got to see to my twin to make sure he's okay. It was years ago, but it's stuck with him all this time.

Swinging a leg over my bike, I follow Styxx over to the grave and squat next to him.

"Why didn't you tell me?"

I sigh and tilt my head up toward the dark sky. "Didn't want to get your hopes up. You got enough shit in your head."

"Doesn't mean you carry the fuckin' burden," he grunts. "Years, brother, fuckin' years we've missed, and now we don't even know the girl we were supposed to protect. Dad would be pissed we didn't take care of her."

"Styxx, we didn't know it was her until it was too late. We were only kids when shit went down. We lost her. Thought she was dead alongside them. Now we got a chance to make things right."

"Yeah, and the first thing we're doing is finding

those people who were supposed to be parents to her," Styxx snarls beating a fist against the dirt.

"Exactly." A grin slides into place on my face. They don't call us Scythe and Styxx for the hell of it. Each of my brothers got their name for being who they are and doing things the way they need to get a job done. "I'll get to work on that, and when I do, brother, we'll make sure they pay along with that dealer."

Nodding, Styxx meets my gaze. "We cool with her being with Hellhound?"

"You saw him earlier just as I did. The way he looks at her, I think it's a good thing for both of them. They both had shit handed to them. They deserve to be happy."

"Right, then let's get out of here and get started on finding the fuckers. I'm not waiting," Styxx mutters and stands. I follow suit and quirk a brow waiting for him to finish. "And don't think you ain't getting out of telling me what the fuck was in your head about going to Finnegan without talking to me first."

I grin and shake my head. "Don't worry. I'll be sure to fill you in later." I slap him on the shoulder and smirk. Together we head for our bikes, and I motion to my brothers, we're heading out. As a whole, they pull up next to us.

"You good?" Daemon asks, eyes going between the two of us.

"Yeah." Styxx nods and blows out a breath before grinning sinisterly. "Who's up for a night out?"

Beast and Ghost both smirk maliciously.

"Fuck yeah, what do you have in mind?" Daemon quirks a brow.

"A little hunting before the hounds of hell are set free for the hunt," I answer, straddling my bike. "Got three people on the list, and I'm sure we'll find them without a problem."

"What we gonna do after we do get hold of them?" Ghost questions.

"We've gotta find some answers, and we got a brother who claimed Isabelle in front of us at the table tonight. He doesn't get a piece of the action. He finds out. We'll all pay the price." Styxx shakes his head. We all know what he means.

The reason they call Hellhound by his road name is he's like a hound with a bone and has no problem feeling the fire.

These dumbasses are fucked.

CHAPTER 10

ISABELLE

The sun is shining through the window as I wake up to find myself in the embrace of warm arms holding me close. I sigh in the contentment of being held. I haven't felt this safe in my entire life.

Yesterday after the guys left to go meet in the other room, I spent some time with Ivy and Sutton. Stella immediately took her leave. I'm guessing she didn't want to talk about whoever she's got a date with. I don't blame her. I've learned she keeps her personal life tight-lipped and doesn't talk much about it.

Ivy and Sutton thankfully didn't grill me on what happened. But it won't take long for them to dive into it. I'm sure they're biding time.

Once I came to the room, exhaustion took over, and I changed into one of Hellhound's tees. I didn't even know when Hellhound came in or that he'd climbed into bed with me. Guess you can say the last few days I haven't slept all too well.

With a sigh of contentment, I snuggle deeper into his hold and relax further. A lot has happened, and I can't get what he said yesterday or what he did to my body out of my head.

I don't fuckin' hate you. It's the opposite. I stayed away so I wouldn't do anything you're not ready for. But that all ends now. You're mine.

More than that, he said, "When you trust me with your story, I'll give you mine. Until then, I'm not answering that question."

Hellhound wants me to be his. Wants me to trust in him.

Then there's the way he looked at me before going into church with his brothers—the sweet touch of his fingers stroking against my skin. I already know I can trust him. I'm just scared and don't know how to tell him.

Hellhound is a man who knows who he is. Knows what he wants. And what he wants in life. I can see it for myself. He's the type of guy who, when he sees it, goes for it. Nothing holds him back when he makes a decision on what he's going to do.

For instance, he's claiming me as his woman.

My heart flutters as a thought crosses my mind. I fell for him before I even realized it had happened. It doesn't help that we're both two scarred souls—perfect for each other, but I still don't feel enough for him. What about what those women were talking about?

"I swear you're thinking loud enough I can hear your mind ticking over whatever the fuck it is."

A shiver radiates up and down my spine, going straight between my legs. I bite my lower lip and roll to face Hellhound, putting my hands flat against his bare chest. I lift my gaze to find him watching me through sleep-filled eyes. But I also see the lingering lust in those dark orbs of his.

I think back to how he didn't push himself on me when he gave me what he did. He didn't even try to get me to do anything to him in order to return the favor. Instead, he held me and said . . . oh my . . .

Before I can chicken out, I slide my hands up his chest and wrap them around Hellhound's neck. I lean into him and press my lips to his. He tenses for all of a second and takes over. Everything goes wild with his fingers roaming over my body. One minute I'm dressed in panties and his tee, the next, I'm stripped to nothing, and Hellhound is between my legs using his mouth.

"Asher," I moan, gripping the sheet.

Hellhound uses his tongue and twirls it around, causing my body to light up as it did yesterday for him.

But unlike yesterday, I want more. More of him. And not just his mouth and fingers.

"Asher, please . . ." I pant.

Hellhound lifts his head, his fingers toying with my entrance. "What do you need, *Críona*? What do you want?"

"You."

"I'm right here, Bells."

I part my lips on a breath and grind against his fingers.

"Tell me, *Críona*, what do you need."

"I need you inside me."

Hellhound doesn't waste a moment longer. He lifts himself over me and then reaches into the nightstand next to the bed. Pulling out a condom, I watch in fascination as he rips the foil open and then slides the latex over his length.

With one look down, my eyes widen, and I gasp at the girth of his cock. I can't help but compare him to Dexter, who had a very small dick . . . Hellhound, on the other hand, has a massive one, and I fear it won't fit.

"*Críona?*"

I meet his gaze as he lines himself up and presses at my entrance.

"You sure about this?" he asks, rubbing the tip against my wetness and leaning down until we're nose to nose.

"Yes." I nod and curve my hands around his shoulders. "I want you."

"After this, Bells, no going back. You're mine, and that's it. I'm not gonna let you go."

"I thought you said I already was yours," I breathe, looking deep into his eyes.

He lifts his head slightly and pushes his hips forward, his cock slipping an inch inside me. "Yeah, *Críona*, I said that, but after I sink into your pussy all of you belongs to me. You understand what I'm saying?"

Oh my.

I'm not sure, but I think I get the gist of what he's saying, and I have to admit to myself it feels nice. Hellhound, I've seen firsthand, doesn't show emotion. Or he didn't. Not with his brothers or anyone else. Him taking me means he wants me.

"I understand."

I barely get the words past my lips before Hellhound slams his lips to mine and thrusts halfway. He pulls almost all the way out only to sink into the hilt. We both groan into each other's mouths, our tongues dancing together.

I swear it feels as if Hellhound takes me to another universe when he starts moving inside me, driving me deeper into a world I never imagined existed.

The feel of him inside me is magnificent, and when my release builds to the point of no going back, I dig my nails into Hellhound's shoulders and cry out against his mouth.

"That's it, *Críona*. Fuck, you feel so good," he

groans against my lips and lifts himself up to pick up the pace. Thrusting fast now, he throws me directly into another orgasmic bliss only to join me.

I focus on his face, loving the look he's giving me. One that's sweet yet dominating at the same time. I don't know exactly how to explain it other than that. It's as if he's marking this moment as me being his in every way.

And I must agree with him. I'm his. I think I've been his since the moment we first met.

Hours after Hellhound and I woke up, and we did the deed, we did it three more times. This is before we showered and did it in there as well. I'm finding Hellhound to be insatiable. I love it, though. My body right now feels like it were rubbery, and I can barely do anything but lay in his bed with him behind me.

Unfortunately, we had to get up. Angel wants to talk to me, and from the sound of his voice through the door, he seems off. I just didn't understand the reason for this.

Hellhound guides me out of his room, his hand wrapped around my shoulders, keeping me next to him. Together we enter the main room of the clubhouse.

I lick my bottom lip nervously at the number of people in the room.

"Um, is everything okay?" I whisper the question, but I'm unsure if I want the answer.

Angel looks to me, then to Scythe and Styxx. His gaze then comes to Hellhound. "We gotta talk," he says, then brings his gaze back to me. "First, we gotta talk to you."

Hellhound tenses next to me and pulls me tighter.

"What's going on?" I ask, glancing around the room.

"Sit down, sweetheart," Angel murmurs motioning to a chair near him.

I notice Ivy and Sutton move in, both with looks of concern.

"Okay, now I'm freaking out," I mutter but walk over and plant myself in the chair. Hellhound moves in behind me, putting himself directly at my back.

"Right," Reaper says. Stepping forward, he jerks his chin to Scythe and Styxx.

Scythe takes a breath and moves in close, and squats down in front of me while holding a folder in my direction.

"You need to see this," he mutters quietly.

With a shaking hand, I take it from him, but before I open it, he speaks up again.

"That folder contains information on you . . ."

I suck in a breath, not liking where he's taking this.

"When I say information. I mean, I know everything there is to know about you."

I'm sure no one misses my wince.

"But what I'm sure you don't know is when you were fifteen months old, you were kidnapped and taken from your family," he announces, causing me to widen my gaze. "What you also don't know is Styxx and me are the brothers you were taken from."

Oh my God.

Mother of information overload.

I don't know what to do with this.

Brothers? I have brothers? And I was kidnapped?

God, can my life for once just be easy and not be filled with drama.

CHAPTER 11

HELLHOUND

"Why are you telling me this now?"

The sound of Isabelle's voice trembling goes straight to my gut. From the way everyone was acting when we stepped into the room, I should have known something wasn't right. Shit, I should've stopped it before they could tell her.

Isabelle's been through a lot of shit in the last god fucking knows how long.

"Because you deserve to know the truth," Styxx answers. "You deserve to not go through another day without knowing you weren't born to those fucked up people."

He had a point. She did deserve to know that, but I would've preferred to be the one to tell her. At least ease her into the knowledge, rather than outright inform her of what they found.

"This is a lot to take in," she whispers, breathlessly stands, turns away from the room, and tilts her head back to look at me. "I . . . I need time. I'm going to go back to your room."

I nod and cup the side of her face. "I'll come check on you soon as I can."

Isabelle gives me a sad look and looks away, steps back, and starts passed me to walk back in the direction of my room. I keep my gaze locked on her backside until she's out of sight.

Fuck me.

Just thirty minutes ago, I'd been deep inside her. From the moment we woke up, she gave me the best gift—her body. We spent the morning fucking. Now that shit is tainted with this bullshit.

I turn my focus back to my brothers and glare at both Styxx and Scythe. "What the fuck are you two thinking?"

"Brother, cool it," Angel mutters calmly.

I whip my dark gaze to him and curl my lip in frustration. "You want me to cool it? What the fuck? I get shits real, but did anyone think of the pain she's been through and what this is going to do to her? Fuck."

"We knew what we were doing," Scythe grunts and straightens to his full height.

"Ivy, why don't you and Sutton go check on her?" Reaper suggests stepping between my brothers and me.

Ivy nods and looks between all of us, but it is Sutton who speaks up.

"I wish you would have come to us first before telling Isabelle. You might have just found that out and wanted her to know. That's great and all, but remember something, you don't know Isabelle like we do. You also think you might know, but you don't know the pain she's been through. Shit, she doesn't even know we know. However, she'd run and hide as she's doing now if she did. We know the truth because she can't hide anything from us. Not really. We all start drinking. She opens up."

"I hope this doesn't set her back," Ivy whispers and waddles toward Reaper. "I don't know what you all are doing, but I also don't want to lose one of my best friends. She's my family."

"Precious, I'm not going to let you lose your family," my Prez mutters, his gaze gentle but the tone of his voice annoyed. "And nothings gonna happen to her . . . besides, she's got her own ol' man who'll look out for her."

Ivy nods and looks at me. "Don't hurt her."

"Not gonna happen," I grunt.

"I believe you." She smiles and moves to Reaper

and kisses him before she and Sutton follow where Isabelle disappeared to.

I refocus on my brothers and plant my hands on my hips. "Someone want to start talking?"

"We got special guests out at the hunting cabin," Angel announces, a glint of anger flashing in his eyes. "Styxx, Scythe, Daemon, Beast, and Ghost went hunting last night. They brought back some morsels for us all to slice into."

Well shit.

Glancing at them, a malicious smirk falls into place, seeing where they're taking this. "I get first dibs."

"As her ol' man, yeah. I'm calling seconds," Angel grumbles, flexing his hands and cracking his knuckles.

"Then let's do this . . . so I can get back to Isabelle and see where her head's at."

Styxx moves and comes to stand in front of me. "I don't have a say in this shit cause her life is hers, and she's just coming back into ours, but don't fuck her over."

I blink, clench my jaw and simply stare at my brother without speaking.

"We know you won't," Styxx states, a look of misery taking over. "But it had to be said because it's what our dad would have wanted. We lost years with our sister doing the whole brotherly bond bullshit and scaring off boyfriends."

"I get it," I mutter inwardly, flinching as the memory of the night Stella was attacked tries to come forward.

As a whole, we all head outside and head to the back of the area clubhouse and to the ATVs we keep back there. In no time, we make our way to the hunting cabin.

I'm the first to step through, only to come to a stop. I glance around the room, not seeing but one body in the middle strung up.

Dexter's.

"What the fuck?" I snarl, curling my lip and scanning the rest of the cabin.

My brothers fill in behind me one by one. The tension filling the room is nearly overwhelming.

"Thought you said you had three," I mutter, looking at Dexter's dead body.

"We did," Daemon answers. "Don't know how they did it. Fucker's escaped but killed the dealer before going. Shit."

"Let's get back to the clubhouse," Reaper says, already heading back out the door. "Something's not sitting right with me. Get the prospects to clean this shit up."

I follow after Reaper, completely in agreement with him. Those druggies got away killing the dealer before going. Something about that smells off. I know a drug addict will do anything for their next fix but fuck me if I can figure this shit out right now.

My only concern at the moment is getting back to the clubhouse and making sure Isabelle is safe. Then I gotta see where her head's at. After that, I'll help her work through things and get her to relax.

CHAPTER 12

HELLHOUND

Two Weeks Later...

"How do two fuckin' druggies disappear into thin air?" I growl, slamming the wrench down on the workbench. I've been out here in the garage off to the side of the clubhouse working on a restoration project. Ghost, Beast, and Tombstone decided to join me. Mostly to get away from the girls inside. Juniper, Josephine, and Everleigh were all visiting. While two of those women aren't bad to be around, they're actually cool. One of them, we all know who, gets on our nerves.

"Brother, cool it," Ghost mutters, narrowing his gaze. "We're all looking for the fuckers. You know that. Shit, I get this is some stressful shit. But you gotta keep your calm. Otherwise, we'll end up having to lock you down, Hellhound, and I know you don't want that to happen."

"No one's lockin' me down," I sneer, shooting him a glare, then level my look on each of my brothers. "I just don't like this shit. Dexter's dead. We didn't get to ask him questions, and I sure as fuck didn't get to make him suffer for what he did to Bells."

"We'll find the druggies, and we'll make them talk. Find the answers to give to Isabelle," Tombstone states, crossing his arms over his chest, making himself look even bigger than he already is.

I nod and blow out a breath and look to the opening leading to the outside. "It bugs the shit out of me not knowing where these fuckers are hiding."

"I think it's getting to all of us," Beast grunts, jerking his chin up in agreement. "You see Scythe and Styxx?"

"Yeah, they're stressing the fuck out. Styxx even called Finnegan himself, and you know he doesn't like his cousin in club shit," Tombstone responds.

"Who would? Finnegan is a crazy fucker, but he's agreed to a sitdown that's supposed to be happening tomorrow," I add and check the time. Seeing it's nearly six, I mutter a curse. "I've got to get going. I'm riding out, swinging by the hospital, checking on Stella, then got to go grab the food. I told Isabelle we'd do something tonight. No way I'm taking her out."

Tombstone chuckles, and Ghost quirks a brow.

"You ever gonna get shit straight between you and Stella?" Beast asks cautiously.

I shrug in response. "Don't know. What I do know is that along with making sure Isabelle stays safe, I've got a sister who needs looking after."

Tombstone stills at my announcement. With everything going on, I haven't had the chance to fill them in on what Connor told me about the marriage contract. It hasn't been imperative that they know anything about it yet. But the longer it takes for my cousin to get back to me, the more I start to think of something else. Connor isn't one for delaying in getting something done, and I know he doesn't want to break alliances while starting a war.

The way of life in the mafia relies on alliances and networking. Most hold their truths together through marriages between families. My father lucked out and left the life with our grandfather's blessing since our uncle didn't mind being head of the house. It worked for him, and my dad wasn't the suit and tie kinda guy. He preferred his Harley and taught me to be the same.

"You wanna elaborate on that?" Tombstone asks, his brows meeting as he frowns.

"Not much to know at the moment. Just that there's a marriage contract for my little sister, and I'm not letting her go through with it. She doesn't know about it, and I want to keep it that way. While doing that, I'll keep her safe," I retort grimly.

"How about you handle taking care of your ol' lady, and I'll keep an eye on your sister?" Ghost suggests.

"We'll all help in taking care of her. Make sure nothing happens." Tombstone nods. "She's become a good friend of Sutton's, and I'm not about to have my ol' lady pissed."

I smirk and shake my head. "Right, you wouldn't want Sutton cutting you off."

"Fuck, no, I don't want her cuttin' me off. Like she would anyways." The corner of his lip tilts up as he grins.

The four of us close up the garage while Beast and Ghost both agree to take two shifts in looking out for Stella. We'd get someone else to take the next two after them.

Out of the corner of my eye, something moves, catching my attention, but when I spin on my heel to head in that direction, it's gone.

"Tombstone, get Ghoul and Goblin to do a trek through the woods. Not just the outer perimeter," I mutter quietly for only him to hear me. My guts telling me something ain't right.

Tombstone nods, and we head for the clubhouse.

The moment we enter, I groan and wish I'd stayed outside cause the first thing to hit my ears is Juniper's annoying voice. The woman's only saving grace is

Isabelle. If it weren't for her being one of my woman's friends, I'd have told her to kick rock the first time I met her. She gets on my ever-loving mind with her attention-seeking.

Meeting Isabelle's smile, I move straight to where she's lounging between Sutton and Everleigh on the couch. I lean down and press a kiss to the top of her head.

"You ready for food, Bells?" I ask, straightening.

She gives me a shy smile, blushes, and bites her lower lip as she nods.

What the fuck is up with blushing? Better yet, the biting of her lower lip? She damn well knows that goes straight to my dick every time.

I open my mouth to ask her about it when, to our right, I hear a sharp gasp and glass breaking. I whip my head in the direction to see Ivy staggering slightly as she cries out in pain.

"Reaper," I roar, calling for my Prez while rushing to Ivy's side along with Tombstone and Daemon.

Reaper and Angel come running. Reaper's eyes widen when he sees Ivy and quickens his pace.

"I got you, Precious," he mutters and lifts her in his arms.

"I'll get the truck," Angel states, moving for the doors.

Everything seems to go in a blur of motion in a moment.

Isabelle comes up next to me, and I wrap an arm around her shoulders, pulling her into my side.

"Guess our plans changed, ugh?" she whispers, leaning her head against me.

I glance down at her and grin. "Yeah, I guess they have. But don't worry, I'll make it up to you later."

"I'll hold you to it." She smiles brightly. "Now, let's go see if Ivy and Reaper are going to have a boy or girl."

CHAPTER 13

ISABELLE

We've been sitting around the waiting room for hours without any news on what's going on with Ivy or the baby. The prospects went out and brought back some drinks and burgers from the burger place down the road. They also had a crap ton of fries and onion rings.

In the past two weeks, if I wasn't in the sight of Hellhound or one of my brothers—I'm still trying to get used to the fact I have siblings—the prospects have an eye on me. Ghoul sat down with me a few days after they moved me out of my apartment. He apologized and said he wouldn't be making that mistake again. He and Goblin both, I can tell, are taking earning their patch seriously. Though Gremlin, a newer prospect, seems to try and think his shit don't stink.

So much has happened, and if not for Ivy, Sutton, Angel, and best of all, Hellhound, I wouldn't have been able to get my head on straight. It's been a lot to deal with coming to terms with Styxx and Scythe being my big brothers, but I have questions I want answered.

The entire evening Hellhound has stuck close to me. I know he doesn't like the fact I'm out in the open away from the clubhouse, considering all that's gone down and the unknown still out there. He told me about my brothers getting Dexter and my so-called parents. He also informed me that Dexter is no longer a threat to me. But the other two were gone before he got to the hunting cabin, and no one knows how they got out of there.

I keep racking my brain with who could've helped them, but I'm not sure who. They had a lot of junky friends who would be around all the time. Maybe I should've paid more attention to them, and I'd be able to help. I can't, though. I did my best to stay out of the way and far from all of those people. I didn't want anything to do with them.

Hellhound moves, drawing my attention to him as he sits in the seat next to me and pulls me into his arms. "You okay, Bells?"

I nod, tilt my head back and look at him. "Yes, I'm just worried about Ivy. They've been in there for a while, and Reaper hasn't come out with updates, and no one's telling us anything."

"She's good, *Críona*," he says, stroking a hand through my hair. Leaning in, he presses a tender kiss to my lips. "Reaper would tear the whole place down by now if she wasn't."

This is true. Reaper absolutely adores his woman. Just before her water broke, Everleigh and Josephine made a joke about how protective the man is of Ivy. Juniper had made a remark about it, and we all brushed it aside. Knowing Juniper as we all do, we get she's high maintenance even if she likes to get muddy. She prefers the attention to be on her. It's just how she was raised to be. Her mom and dad spoiled her to be that way, and we all ignored it. Well, for the most part.

"Yeah," I whisper and lay my head against his shoulder.

Another hour or so passes before Reaper finally comes through the doors, looking exhausted, but he's smiling brightly.

"How is she? The baby?" Everleigh asks, clearly anxious and worried as we all are about our friend.

"Ivy's good. Had to do a c-section. She's being moved to recovery now. Babies are going to NICU," Reaper breaths out heavily and runs a hand over the top of his head.

"Wait, did you just say babies?" Angel asks cautiously, brows furrowed.

Reaper drops his hand and grins. "Yeah, a boy and girl, Paxton and Sage."

"Oh shit." Tombstone chuckles. "Did you know?"

"Our little girl was hiding behind her brother the whole time," Reaper answers and glances around the room. "I know you all want to see her and the twins, but she needs to rest, and I've gotta run between. So go on home, get some sleep."

"I'm not leaving you and Ivy alone," Angel mutters, crossing his arms. "I sure as hell ain't leaving my niece and nephew unprotected. Not when shit's going down, and you know it."

Reaper stiffens and glares at our VP. "Right, then pick a few brothers to stay, and the rest of you go on for the night."

I glance at Hellhound and whisper quietly for only him to hear. "You can stay if you want." With him being the SAA of the club, I know he's probably needed.

"*Críona*, I'm not letting you be far from me unless I have to, and that goes for now as well. Got me?"

I nod, seeing the glittery glint shining in his eyes. "Okay."

The members of the club huddle together for a brief chat while I hug my friends and tell them I'll get with them later. Juniper gives a look and then makes a huffing sound. I don't know what's going on with her, but she's been moodier than normal, well prissier.

By the time Hellhound and I finally get out of there,

I'm exhausted, ready to fall on my face. I think when we get to the clubhouse, I'm going to sleep for days on in, though I know it'll only be a few hours before I get up so I can get back up here and to my friend.

———

Hellhound strokes his fingers along my bare side. His tender touch is something in the past few weeks I've gotten used to. He can be sweet and loving while inside me, but he can also be rough and wild. Both, I absolutely love. I've never done any of what he's done with me—the positions, exploring all he's shown me.

With not having to fear Dexter anymore, I think it's easier to be me. I'm able to find my way without the thought of looking over my shoulder. I'm not scared out of my mind that I won't be able to cover my 'parents' debt and end up at the hands of that monster.

"Bells?" Hellhound mutters, pulling me out of my head before I can fully go down that dark path.

I tilt my head back on his shoulder and meet his gaze. "Yeah?" I whisper for some reason, not wanting to be loud.

"You okay?" he asks—his deep baritone going straight to my chest, clenching tightly.

"Do you like kids?" I blurt out without meaning to. The moment the question slips past my lips, my eyes widen, and I tense as Hellhound's arms tighten around me.

He turns us until we're both lying on our sides facing each other. Hellhound raises a hand to cup the side of my face and strokes my hair out of the way. "Yeah, *Críona*, I like kids." Sliding his hand down, he brushes his thumb over my lip. "What about you?"

"I . . . I, um, I never really thought about it. I mean . . ." I suck in a nervous breath, realizing he didn't ask me if I wanted them but if I liked them. "I mean, yes, I like kids. I never thought about having any, but that well, you know. I feared never being able to take care . . ."

"I know what you mean, Bells," he interrupts me, grinning. "And I'm gonna explain something to you. Growing up, I had great parents. My mom was a stay-at-home woman who enjoyed spending her time with her son and daughter. My dad worked hard. He was a biker, but he didn't belong to a club, though he was friends with the Satan Keepers. He simply liked living his life the way he wanted to. They died years ago. I got guardianship of Stella and started prospecting for the club."

My heart hurts for him that he lost his parents.

"You asked me about the scar on my face, and I'm gonna tell you. It was because I failed in protecting my sister."

I gasp, shocked at what he's admitted.

"Asher," I whisper, cupping the side of his face and brushing my fingers along his scar.

"Long time ago, Isabelle," he mutters. "For a long time, I was pissed with Stella. She didn't listen to me when I told her not to do something. She did it anyway, and the result of it ended with her getting hurt and me killing a fucker, but not before he got one good shot at me. That shot being slicing the side of my face in with a hunting knife."

Oh no.

"So, I never thought of having any kids myself, *Críona*." He slides his hand into my hair and holds me still. "But that was before you. What you need to do, though, Bells, is know that I want a life with you. One that includes you as my ol' lady, wearing my patch, my ring, and carrying my kid inside you. It ain't gonna be tomorrow, but soon enough. I learned a lot from my folks growing up, but the hardest lesson I got from them is life is fuckin' short. Now you think you can handle all that?"

I nod without hesitation, licking my bottom lip. His words swirl around in my head, searing themselves in place. If it were anyone else but Hellhound, I might go running from him a mile a minute. However, this is Hellhound, and he knows the worst of me. So who cares if he killed a man. That guy must have deserved it. I might not know everything about this man, but I know he's not a cold-blooded killer. Everything he does is with purpose, and he calculates his move before doing anything.

"Need words, *Críona*," he says, pressing his lips against mine for a chaste kiss.

"I can handle everything you said," I whisper truthfully.

Hellhound smirks and repositions us, rolling so I'm on my back, and he's on top of me, his body cradled between my legs. I suck in a breath when he slips inside my already wet entrance.

"You're so fuckin' beautiful but more so when you get that sweet look on your face when I fill you with my cock."

Oh my.

I run my hands up his arms and wrap them around his shoulders while I tip my hips for him to sink deeper inside me. "Asher," I moan, savoring the feel of him.

"Yeah, *Críona*." The gruffness of his voice sends a shiver down my spine.

With a slow thrust, Hellhound takes his time loving me in a way he's not done before. Tears well in my eyes at how sensual it feels. It's beautiful in a way I never understood sex could be. The two of us come together, our mouths brushing against each other's as our releases take over.

Still inside me, Hellhound repositions us, so I'm on top of him, my head to his chest.

"Sleep, *Críona*," he murmurs, pressing a kiss to the top of my head.

I smile, release a breath of contentment and close my eyes. It doesn't take me long to do as he orders. I drift off to sleep murmuring something I didn't even realize I said. "I love you."

CHAPTER 14

HELLHOUND

One week later . . .

"Yo, Hellhound," Scythe calls from across the bay.

I tilt my head in his direction and furrow my brow, seeing Styxx, Angel, Tombstone, and Daemon behind him.

Over the past week, we've somewhat gotten back into the swing of things. The girls are still on lockdown, not allowed to go anywhere without someone on them. Ivy's at the clubhouse with the twins. My Prez has barely left her side, making sure she's got everything she needs. Along with helping her take care of the twins. Meaning we were all leaving him the fuck alone for the time being. His focus is needed elsewhere.

Sutton's been staying at the clubhouse without complaint, helping Reaper and Ivy where she can but also working from her computer. Isabelle, though, needed something to do, and the club gave it to her—with Ivy not getting upset. We got her to start working in the office at the garage. Ivy even suggested the two of them work in there together, so it's not all on one or the other.

None of us cared, long as we didn't have to do the office shit. We're not ones for filing.

"What?" I ask, glancing behind the men coming my way to the windows leading to the office and seeing my woman standing at the file cabinet—the top drawer open.

"We got something," Angel answers through clenched teeth.

I straighten from under the hood of the car I'm working on and frown, glancing between the four men. "What do you mean y'all got something?" The tension radiating off my brothers hits me, and I feel it in my gut. Whatever it is they found can't be good. Not in the least.

"Finnegan went looking into both Isabelle's 'parents,'" Styxx states, spitting out the last word as if it were a bad taste in his mouth. "Found those fuck ups aren't just druggies. They have connections. Ones that used them to hide our little sister for years."

"What connection?" I cross my arms, bracing for

more.

"You ever hear of a group, the Scarlet Needles?" Daemon asks.

I shake my head in answer and quirk a brow.

"Well seems these druggies are related to someone who used to work with our father. Finnegan found the link, and I went with it," Scythe states, his eyes burning with anger. "I followed it, and you know how our dad was a surgeon. Well, the Scarlet Needles is a black-market organ trade. They wanted him to come work for them. When he found out what they did, he declined. That's the reason behind the deaths. Does Isabelle have any scars on her? Maybe looking like a surgical scar."

I nod, thinking about the one where she said they took her appendix out when she was nine. "Yeah," I answer and tell them what she told me.

"Fuck," Styxx snarls. "We need to get her checked out, see what they took. I highly doubt it was her appendix."

"I'll call Stella and ask what we can do about finding out," I mutter without thinking. I still haven't talked to her. But it's time we finally put the fucking past behind us and move on with our lives.

"Right," Angel mutters, nodding. "Now for the rest of it."

Something about the way he states this rubs me the wrong way. "What?"

"Goblin and Ghoul found something in the woods finally. It's on the far back end. They scoped it out, and it looks like a woman has been hiding out. They set a trap, and low and behold, guess who's fuckin' back?" Angel sneers.

"Claws," Tombstone spits out, curling his lip in hatred.

What the fuck! "Tell me they got the cunt."

"Oh, they got her all right," Styxx smirks sinisterly. "She's now in the cabin whining and pleading for us to let her go. We put Beast on her to keep an eye on her and make sure nothing happens. She's already confessed to helping the druggies escape. And she killed the dealer herself. Though we don't know why yet."

"We need to get to the bottom of all of this shit," I snarl, fisting my hands at my sides. "I'm done with all the bullshit drama and us having to wait to see what the fucks gonna happen next. Were we able to get a location on those two fuckin' druggies?"

"They haven't been back to their place or to Isabelle's. I've been looking into all the different places they could be, but I'm not getting shit all on them. They're ghosts." Scythe mutters, shaking his head.

"Fuck." I glance behind them and focus on my woman. "Let's finish the day out, then deal with what we can for now. Give her one day of normal," I say, jerking my chin toward Isabelle working in the office.

"She deserves it," Styxx mutters quietly.

Since Reaper and Ivy's twins were born, Styxx and Scythe have been getting closer to Isabelle and trying to be the brothers they didn't get to be.

Shit.

They even tried threatening me plenty of times, telling me to do right by her. But if they knew just how much she means to me, they wouldn't even have to question it. Then again, Isabelle doesn't know. However, I inwardly grin, remembering the night I told her about how I got the scar on my face, and she still took me as I am telling me as she drifted to sleep that she loved me. I don't even know if she remembers those three little words spilling from her mouth.

I'll give her this time to have normal. Then after I get this shit dealt with, I'll make sure she's only ever got normal to fill her days.

Angel, Daemon, and I stay behind to finish up and close up the garage together before heading back to the clubhouse. Isabelle shuts down the office and locks up as we finish closing the bays.

After our talk, Scythe, Styxx, and Tombstone went to the clubhouse to inform Reaper what's going down at Angel's command.

My eyes follow my woman making her way to me, her smile aimed at me.

"You enjoy working in the office today?" I ask, curling my arm around her when she's close enough.

"Yeah, you guys suck at paperwork," she states sternly.

My brothers and I throw our heads back, bursting into laughter at her comment.

"Sweetheart, you don't know the half of it." Angel chuckles.

"Let's get out of here." Daemon grins. "You can tell Ivy about that shit at the clubhouse."

"Please don't." Angel snorts. "She'll have a conniption, and then Reaper will get on our case."

I shake my head, grinning as we all head for our bikes, knowing he's right. Reaper will blow if Ivy gets worked up because she'll demand to come back to work to fix shit back up to the way she likes it.

"Don't worry. I won't tell her." Isabelle giggles. "But don't think I'm not going to put shit back in order and get a little ticked off if things don't stay organized. You think Ivy's bad for it? Um, I'm worse."

"Oh shit, tell me you didn't say that?" Daemon groans.

"Brother, you saw her apartment when you helped pack her up," Angel states, shaking his head. "She's fuckin' OCD like a bitch."

"Hey," Isabelle snaps playfully. "Just because I like

things kept neat and where they're supposed to be doesn't mean I'm OCD."

I give her a look quirking my brow, "*Críona* wanna try that again?"

Isabelle rolls her eyes, smiling brightly. "Whatever."

My brothers chuckle, and we all move to straddle our bikes. With my attention on Isabelle, I fuck up by not focusing more on our surroundings.

The sound of a gun going off rings in my ears as a pain unlike any other hits my stomach. Isabelle screams and touches where I'd been shot.

Angel and Daemon move in, cursing.

I groan, allowing Isabelle to take some of my weight, but I don't give it all to her. Daemon wraps an arm around my waist and helps lower me to the ground while Angel returns fire and covers the rest of us.

"Please be okay," Isabelle cries, lifting a hand to stroke my cheek.

"It's all good, Bells," I mutter, wincing at the pain.

"No, it's not. You're shot." Her breath hitches on a sob.

"Sweetheart, do me a favor and call for an ambulance and back up," Angel calls out over his shoulder as another shot's fired. Angel grunts, telling me he's been hit.

I don't know who the fuck is shooting at us, but whoever it is, they're aiming to take us out.

CHAPTER 15

ISABELLE

No. No. No.

This can't be happening. After doing what Angel tells me to do, I hang up with Tombstone and look from Hellhound to Daemon. He's got his eyes scanning the area, but his hands are pressing against the wound at my man's gut.

Tears spill down my cheeks, and I look around Angel to see past the corner where the shooter is shooting from. Narrowing my gaze, I realize who the attackers are—my parents.

Fucking parents who aren't even my real parents.

What the ever-loving hell?

Stiffly, I stand, ignoring all three men as they tell me to get back down. Hellhound even tried to move, but I was quicker than all of them. I run past Angel straight to my parents and scream. "Stop. Just stop. Leave me alone."

My mother curls her lip up and shakes her head. "You are supposed to take care of me. Of him. You're ours, and you are meant to take care of us. Pay our debts. We took you in, and this is how you repay us."

At her screeching words, my stomach turns, and it's all I can do to keep from puking right then and there. Something inside me flips, and I can't control my movements. I launch myself at her taking her to the ground. I feel hands at my shoulders trying to yank me off the woman, but I shrug them off. I repeatedly slam my fake mother's head against the concrete sidewalk. Sirens are heard, though I'm not paying attention.

One minute I'm beating on the hateful woman. The next, I'm lifted off her. "Let me go," I screech, kicking and screaming.

"Calm down, *Críona*," Hellhound growls, turning me to face him. He shoves my face in his chest just as two shots ring in the air and ring in my ears.

Suddenly everything goes eerily quiet for a moment.

"Fuck," Angel mutters next to us, and Daemon moves in. "We ain't gonna be able to hide this shit."

"Nope, but we'll handle it," Hellhound grunts.

"Brother, you're fuckin' bleeding all over your woman," Daemon states.

"I don't care," I mumble, holding on to my man, hoping I'm not hurting him.

"Isabelle, we're gonna need you to keep quiet and go with what we say," Angel mutters sternly, getting my attention.

I lift my head and narrow my gaze on him. "What's that supposed to mean, huh?"

"We gotta handle the cops, and there's gonna be questions . . ."

"I don't care about the questions. If they want to ask them, let them. The truth is self-defense. Better yet, they turned on each other, shooting one another at the same time. Like I say, I don't give a shit. What I do care about happening is you and Hellhound are taken care of first and foremost."

"Sweetheart," Angel says gently.

"No." I shake my head and step away from Hellhound to look at both of them. My man and the man who became like a brother before I knew I had real ones. "You both could've died," I yell and look at Daemon. "All three of you could have. Angel and Hellhound were hit. You could've been in the same boat. If it wasn't for me, none of this would've happened."

"*Críona*, calm down," Hellhound tries.

"No. No. No." I drop to my knees and cry, wishing I could turn back time. I mean, my man was hit because he stood in front of me. And he's still strong, ignoring the pain to take care of me.

"Brother, I got her," Daemon says, coming to my side and scooping me in his arms. "Calm down, babe. We'll get them taken care of—both of them.

I nod, still crying in his arms.

Everything goes by in warp speed, from the ambulance coming with the police to the trip to the hospital.

Styxx and Scythe stayed close, guarding over me while we waited for Hellhound to get out of surgery. Stella reported that everything was good, and if he woke up after surgery before morning, he'd demand to go home just as Angel is already tried. His wounds were bad, but I still freaked out, and they admitted him for my peace of mind.

Once Hellhound was in a room, they took me to him. I broke into tears, and nothing would stop them. Several of Hellhound's brothers hold me while Stella gives me something to calm down. Not even a moment later, my eyes droop, and I pass out with Daemon's arms around me.

CHAPTER 16

HELLHOUND

Waking up in the hospital is the last place I want to be, but for Isabelle's peace of mind, it's where I'm at.

Fuck.

I can't believe I wasn't paying attention and ended up fucking shot. Between Angel and I, we ended up earning a stay at the hospital. Where I got shot in the gut, he took two bullets. One in the shoulder and another in the side. They were more grazes than anything, but Stella admitted us both for Isabelle's mentality. Stella even ended up giving my woman something for her to relax and sleep after the whole ordeal. It was just easier to get her to calm down.

And right now, I know she's still sleeping, curled into a ball in the chair sitting close to the bed. Both her brothers and several other members of the club tried getting her to leave last night, but she refused. I only know all of this cause after I awoke from surgery, she was there, and Angel reported it to me. He'd been able to keep her from going out of her mind by agreeing to everything and keeping her close.

Last night she kept blaming herself before I passed out, but what she didn't know is I'd do it all over again. For her, I'd sacrifice my life for her—she means that much to me.

I peek at the door as it opens to my little sister stepping inside. Her eyes come straight to the bed, meeting my gaze head-on. I can see the hesitation in them as she comes to a stop. I realize it's time. She needs to stop holding on to the guilt, and I need to do the same. We both need to move on with our lives.

"Come here," I murmur, not wanting to wake Isabelle.

Stella seems apprehensive at first, but in the end, she comes to stand at the side of the bed and shocks the shit out of me by blurting out. "I'm sorry."

I furrow my brow and cock my head slightly. "What are you sorry for?"

"Everything," she breathes dropping her head and fiddling with her fingernails. She's always been like that when nervous, fidgeting with her nails. Our mom used to paint them to keep her from doing that. Stella wouldn't mess them up as much if they were done, but right now, there's no color to them.

"Stella, look at me," I command sternly but keep my tone gentle.

Stella listens, and the tears welling in her eyes tell me this shit between us has gone on way too fucking long.

"Let it go, Twinkle," I state, calling her by a name I've not used in years. It's the one my dad and I gave her when we were kids.

Stella was always known for having this brightness around her. Smiling and laughing at everything. She also had a beautiful heart that just brought a light like no other into a room filled with darkness. After they died, that shimmering light around her disappeared.

"I can't let it go, Asher," she whispers, shaking her head.

"Why?"

Stella sucks in a breath and looks from me to Isabelle, then back to hold my gaze. "I just can't."

"Bullshit, Stella. We gotta let it go. I realize that shit. I fucked up years ago with you and never made it right. You got hurt . . ." I don't miss the sharp breath Stella sucks in and the way she starts shaking. "I know it hurts, Twinkle, to think about it, but the truth is I blame myself for you getting hurt. If I did a better job in making sure you didn't go out that night, nothing would have happened to you, and I took that shit out on you. You're not responsible, and it's time you got that shit out of your head. Let it go and finally live a beautiful life. One you deserve to have."

I wait for my little sister to let that all sink in, and when it does, I open my arms for her. Stella leans down and presses her cheek into the crook of my neck. Wetness hits my skin, but I don't care. This shit between us shouldn't have ever happened, and like Scythe and Styxx, I've also finally got my sister back. Unlike them, though, I could've always had her in my life.

Fuck, I'm a complete and utter dick.

After a few minutes, Stella pulls away and wipes her face clear of all tears.

"You good now?"

Stella nods and gives me a small smile. "Yes."

"Good, then can I get some discharge papers. I want the fuck out of here."

At my comment, she bursts into a fit of laughter, waking Isabelle.

"What's going on?" Isabelle asks, her face going from panic to relaxed seeing it's just Stella. "Everything okay?"

"Sorry, *Críona*," I murmur and motion for her to come to the bed.

"I'll, um, I'll get the papers situated, and you both can go home and relax. And I mean relax, Asher, no screwing around. You're lucky that bullet didn't hit anything major, and I mean lucky. Not as in because you're Irish, so don't even try me. Take it easy, and I'll check on you there when I get off."

I roll my eyes at my sister's comment. It's a joke she knows Connor and I have between us. We used to do some crazy stunts as teenagers, and Uncle Ryan said we had the luck of the Irish to keep us from getting hurt or in trouble.

"Whatever, Stella, just get me the fuck out of here."

She rolls her eyes and leaves my room, closing Isabelle and me in alone together.

"Are you sure you should leave here?" Isabelle asks, the panic starting to take hold of her again.

"Bells, I'm okay," I tell her and reach up to stroke her cheek. "You can nurse me back to health at the clubhouse. But I'm telling you, I'm good."

"But . . ."

"Fuckin' love you, *Críona*," I murmur, changing the subject to get her mind off me leaving the hospital.

Isabelle's eyes widen, and she gasps. "You love me?"

"Said it, didn't I?" I smirk, sliding a hand into her mess of hair. "You mean the world to me, woman, and I want you to know I'll do whatever it takes to keep you safe. If I hadn't been standing where I was when that first bullet went off, you wouldn't be here now. Fuck, Bells, I'd give my life for yours any day. Though that shits over with, and you've got nothing to worry about anymore." And I meant it. She didn't have anything to worry about anymore. Those druggies are dead, killed by me, Daemon, and Angel.

"It's over," she whispers.

"Yeah, it's done. But that doesn't mean your not in trouble for that stunt you pulled by going after them," I growl, narrowing my eyes on her. "I'm thinking that earned you ten spankings."

Isabelle's eyes glaze over with a heated look that goes straight to my dick.

I've learned my woman likes to be spanked. Just as much as she likes taking me anyway I give it.

Fuck, this shit is gonna suck not being able to do what I want. Guess I'll have to get creative because there's no damn way I'm going without her sweet pussy until this wound heals.

CHAPTER 17

ISABELLE

Three Weeks Later . . .

Nightmares have been waking me every night, and I'm never able to get back to sleep. Worse I wake up screaming, causing all those in the clubhouse to wake with me. I feel horrible about it, but no one holds it against me. Everything, I suppose, finally caught up to me, and I'm reliving everything through my dreams.

Hellhound was released the day after he was shot, and they removed the bullet. Same for Angel though he didn't have to have a bullet pulled out of him. Both of them suggested I speak to someone about my dreams. My man told me he didn't care if it was a professional, a support group, someone at the clubhouse, him, or a friend—just as long as I talked about what my nightmares consist of.

It's not been easy. Honestly, it's hard to do, but I finally started to talk about them with Everleigh, Sutton, and Ivy. Though most of the time, it's Everleigh I talk with just the two of us. She's been able to help me a lot with finding something else to do to take my mind off what happened when Hellhound was shot protecting me. Sometimes she'll take me out into the woods, where we sit and commune with nature. She's not a hippie or anything like that, but she explained to me that getting close to nature helps clear the mind of the toxins filling it. It's why she rides ATVs. I get it, and the last few days have been going out there sitting just inside the tree line to be alone and allow the power of nature to help heal me.

Coming into the clubhouse after spending time outside, I find Hellhound sitting at the bar. I stop just inside the door at the sight of three of the P&Ps surrounding him. All of them have their hands on him. His only saving grace is he doesn't look happy.

"Come on, Hellhound, you know she's not good enough for you," the one called Chops coos.

Hellhound's gaze comes to mine, and I shake my head. I know we haven't really had sex, but that doesn't mean he hasn't gotten off.

"Let's go to your room, and we'll give you what

you need," Fuzzy suggests, running her hands along his chest.

Not wanting to hear any more, I stomp my way toward them and, without thinking, grab Chops and Fuzzy by their hair. Croak yells at me, stepping away from Hellhound as I yank the two back and shove them to the floor.

"What the hell do you think you're doing?"

I narrow my gaze on Croak and then to the other two. "It's not me who should be answering that question but you three."

"Bitch he ain't yours," Chops sneers, clamoring to her feet.

"The fuck you say?" Hellhound snarls standing. He reaches out and tags me around the waist, pulling me close to his side.

"Let me handle this, Asher," I murmur, tilting my head back, letting him know it has to be me to deal with them. If not, they'll keep doing it.

He nods, and I give him a smile of thanks before turning back to the skanks.

"If he's not mine, then why is it I'm in his bed every night, his cock inside me whatever way he wants it, and I sleep curled in his side . . . again, every night?" I seethe, shooting them all with my best glare. "You three and the rest of you skanky twat waffles are nothing more than what they call you pocket pussies. You open your legs and let them do whatever. Shit, I'm just glad I've not had to walk in to find them running a train on you all. That just makes me wanna vomit at the thought. But I wouldn't put it past you dirty bitches to do something like that. And you wonder why you can't lock one down as an ol' man."

"Bitch . . ."

"Don't you call her a bitch," Sutton snaps, coming into the conversation. "Bells is right. You skanks best get with the program. We're fuckin' ol' ladies, and we're not gonna stand for you trying this shit. If a brother has an ol' lady back the fuck off. Especially when it comes to my man."

"And mine," Ivy spits out as she steps forward. "Reaper might not have gotten pussy lately, but that doesn't mean he wants anything to with y'all's snatches. And for the record, Croak, he doesn't want you. He's got my mouth for now, so back the fuck off."

"I did not need to hear that shit," Angel mutters from across the room. "Let's end this shit before I fuckin' puke. P&Ps, learn your place and quit fuckin' around with the ol' ladies. This is the only warning you get. Got me?"

They all nod sharply in response and lower their gazes to the floor.

"Good, now get the fuck out of my sight," Angel growls.

I giggle as they take off, rushing out of the room down the hall leading to their rooms.

"Isabelle," Hellhound murmurs calling my name as he turns me in his arms. "Fuckin' beautiful what you just did. Proud of you for sticking up for yourself and me."

I blush and lean into him as I realize exactly what I said and who I said it in front of.

Hellhound, however, doesn't seem to mind, and I know this because he grips the back of my head and slams his mouth to mine. His tongue slides in between my lips. Then he scoops me into his arms. I know I should tell him to put me down, but he doesn't listen to me.

Taking me to his room, he lays me on the bed and spends the next several hours showing me his appreciation along with telling me how much he loves me.

CHAPTER 18

HELLHOUND

One Week Later...

"Everything in place?" I ask Sutton and Ivy as they turn toward me in the kitchen when I enter.

Ivy smiles and nods while rocking Paxton in her arms. I grin, knowing my Prez has his little girl with him. Both kids have both their parents wrapped around their fingers though Sage is Reaper's little princess, and he's not one for letting her out of his sight. Same with his ol' lady. Though he's good as long as his woman is in the clubhouse, but she steps foot outside, he's on her ass.

"Everything's ready. You just got to get her out

there," Sutton says reassuringly. "And just for the record, she's gonna love it."

I hope she loves it. Shit, I never thought I'd be going out and doing what I did, but I did. After my parents died years ago, they left the insurance policy to Stella and me. I kept all of it except what was needed to pay off bills and whatnot. I offered to use it to pay for my sister's schooling, but our Uncle took care of it. So now I've made an investment with a portion of my share and bought a house not far from here. I've also booked a trip for just Isabelle and me to take. I'm taking her to Ireland to meet my family. I want them to know who she is and what she means to me.

"Go get her tiger," Ivy snickers, nodding to the door. Sutton joins in with giggling.

I sigh and shake my head at both women. I don't know when it happened, but those two, along with Isabelle, have ingrained themselves within this club. Each of them always has someone there to take their back if need be and not just because they're ordered. No, it's because of who they are.

Leaving both women to do their thing, I head in search of Isabelle and find her right away hanging with Angel. If I didn't know the relationship with them was strictly platonic, I might get pissed with how Angel flirts with her. But that's just who the fuck he is.

I close the distance between Isabelle and me and lean down to kiss the side of her neck. "Got somewhere we gotta go," I murmur softly in her ear, not missing the way she shivers in my arms.

"Where's that?" she asks, shifting so she can look over her shoulder at me.

"You'll see." I grin, releasing her to take her hand.

She doesn't respond as I tug her closer and guide her out of the clubhouse and to my bike. I grab her helmet off the handlebars and hand it to her. With ease, she slips it over her head and straps it under her chin while I put my own on.

I straddle my bike and lift the stand after she climbs on behind me and wraps her arms tightly around my waist. I'll never get tired of having her holding on while she's on the back of my bike.

Isabelle was made to ride behind me and to keep her there, I'll do whatever the fuck it takes.

We still have shit to deal with regarding Claws and other shit, but today's about Isabelle, and that shit's for another day. The club voted to keep Claws around for one reason only, and that's information. We need to get that out of her, and we're not killing her until we know she's told us everything. For the time being, she's stuck in a cell that we keep in the basement of the hunting cabin. Out there, no one can hear her screams.

I take the long way to get to our destination, savoring the feel of her behind me. But still, it's way too short of a ride as we pull into the driveway. Shutting the bike down and putting the kickstand down, I unstrap my helmet and tap Isabelle's hands, letting her know to get off.

"Where are we?" she asks as soon as she gets her own helmet off.

I give her a grin and climb off the bike. I take the helmet from her hand and place it on the handlebars.

Turning my full attention to Isabelle, I hook an arm around her waist and drag her flush against my chest, reach down and cup her ass in both my palms. Like she's done so many times before, my woman slides her arms up to wrap them around my neck, knowing what I'm gonna do. I lift her up, so she has no choice but to fold her legs around my waist. I love the feel of her pressing against me like this.

With ease, I carry her up to the house and through the unlocked door.

"Asher?" Isabelle whispers, using my name as she's started doing more often than not. She doesn't care if we're in front of my brothers or not. She claims I'm no longer Hellhound to her. Only Asher. The man who carries both men within him.

If she weren't cute as fuck, I might have a problem with it. Unfortunately, she gets away with a lot of shit, but nothing drastic.

I set her on her feet, keeping a hand around her waist. "Welcome home, Bells," I whisper, stretching an arm out, indicating the inside of the house.

Isabelle's mouth drops, and her eyes widen as she glances from me to look around the house. I think I did pretty good picking a place she'd like. I bought it keeping everything that is Isabelle in mind.

It's a simple ranch-style house, but it's got a bay window in the kitchen, a sunroom off the back where I can see her spending a good about of time. After closing, my brothers and I took out all the windows, replacing them with bulletproof ones, and put in a top-of-the-line security system.

"Y-you . . . you bought a h-house," she stutters, bringing her wide eyes to me. "For me?"

"Yeah, *Críona*, I bought us a house," I answer, reaching up to stroke her cheek with my thumb.

"But . . ."

I lean in and kiss her to keep her from talking since I'm not finished. I press my forehead to hers and hold her close. "I'm not perfect by any means, *Críona*, but no one is. I'm gonna fuck up along the way. That's just the way I am. However, I can say I'll never fuckin' hurt you. You mean the world to me, and I'm not going to go without you in my life. We've both had a shit time of things, and I've sacrificed a lot over the years. This time though, I'm asking you to make a sacrifice by agreeing to not just be with me but to marry me and be mine in every way. I told you a while back that I intended to do that. Now I'm asking."

Isabelle's eyes widen, and her lips part as tears well in her eyes. She nods her head slowly as she answers. "That's not a sacrifice, Asher Ryan, but yes, I'll marry you."

I barely let her finish speaking before capturing her mouth in mine. Holding her in my arms, I drop us to the floor right there in the entrance of our home, where I show her how pleased I am at her agreeing to be mine.

I strip her of her jeans and shirt, rip her panties out of the way, and slide inside her. Isabelle cries out, and I thrust harder, giving her everything she wants. There's nothing more beautiful than watching as she comes unraveled for me.

Within no time, we come together, panting, kissing, and holding on to each other.

Never in my life did I think I'd have something or someone to make my life worth anything, but Isabelle gives that to me, and I'll sacrifice my own life to keep her where she is. At my side. On the back of my bike. Always near me, giving me everything I need to survive to keep going.

EPILOGUE

ISABELLE

Summer is in full swing, and today everyone is relaxing outside after the guys got back from going on a ride. Ivy, Sutton, and I stayed behind to get everything ready for when they returned.

They wanted to have a party, and we spent a good part of the day preparing for it. The guys will cook the meat on the grills, but there's no way they'll do the rest.

While I put together the pasta salad and potato salad, Ivy made her dishes, and Sutton did hers. We all took time keeping an eye on Ivy and Reaper's twins. I love spending time with those two sweethearts. They're adorable and have every last member of the club tied around their finger. Especially Sage. She's the princess, and when she gets older, I feel for anyone who comes near her.

Everleigh, Josephine, and Juniper finally got here about thirty minutes before the guys pulled back in. I knew Everleigh and Josephine were going to be late due to their jobs, but I shouldn't be surprised about Juniper. Over the last few months, I've noticed a change in her, and it's one that makes me feel uncomfortable. Something's up with her, and it's not good.

A set of arms wraps around me from behind, and I relax into the warm body they're attached to while I laugh at Sutton.

"What are y'all laughing at?" Hellhound asks, pressing a kiss to the side of my neck.

I tilt my head back and smile. "Sutton was just telling us about how Tombstone took the news about her being pregnant."

Hellhound smirks and shakes his head before looking at Sutton. "He pass out on you?"

"No, the big jerk freaked and started mumbling about baby-proofing the house," she giggles, "I'm only twelve weeks, and he's going to end up having the whole place bubble wrapped, including me before he or she even gets here."

"You sure it's just one kid?" Ivy snickers.

"Hahahaha." Sutton rolls her eyes, smiling. "According to my ultrasound, it's only showing one baby. So that's what I'm going with. Twins don't run in my family, and I'm hoping they don't in his."

I giggle for a moment before a thought pops into my head, and my eyes nearly pop out of my head.

"What's wrong, *Críona*?" Hellhound asks, feeling me tense.

I whip around to face him, planting my hands on his chest. "What . . . what if we have twins? I don't know if they run in your family . . . but Scythe and Styxx. They're twins. Oh no. I don't think I could handle carrying twins. That would be too much. The thought of one freaks me out, but being responsible for two is way different. I mean, sure, I help with Paxton and Sage, but that's T totally different. They're not ours. I can give them back when they're crying and whatnot."

Hellhound shuts me up by kissing me deeply, then rests his forehead against mine. "You saying what I think you're saying, *Críona*?"

"Um," I breathe, pressing myself closer.

"Yeah, I think you're telling me you got my baby inside you." He grins and pulls me even closer and slams his mouth to mine.

Catcalls and whistles hit my ears. Hellhound lifts his head enough to smile down at me, his eyes glittering with happiness. I know at that moment, even if I were carrying twins, he'd be there for me every step of the way.

STELLA

My heart flutters with pure happiness that finally, my brother has someone in his life that's not a disappointment. For the first time, he can be happy and not worry about a thing. Isabelle's perfect for him.

Years ago, I screwed up by rebelling against him. I can't blame it on anyone or anything. I was simply being stupid. Because of my actions, I lost my brother. Hellhound did what he needed to do for the both of us by sending me away.

I ended up finishing school, going to college, got my medical degree, and now I'm back in his life. I don't want to be a disappointment anymore. I want to find my own happiness, but I don't think it's in the cards for me. Especially now.

But it'll be okay. What's going on in my life will stay that way. No one needs to know. Not about the threats I've been getting. Nor do they need to know about the baby I'm carrying.

Sighing, I rest my hand on my stomach nonchalantly as I scan the party and roll my eyes when I spot Juniper all but latching onto Angel like a leech. I've heard all of her friends tell her to cool it, though she never listens.

Angel, his road name's Dark Angel, but everyone

just calls him Angel because it's easier. I swallow nervously anytime his gaze comes to mine, like now. Only he's got this annoyed look in his eyes. One that tells me he's none too happy about seeing me. I get why and don't blame him.

I wish I could go to him, but I can't. Well, I won't. He's not mine and never will be.

Dropping my gaze from his, I spin on my heel and make my way out of there. I'm not needed to be around. If it weren't for the women who've entered the lives of these men, I wouldn't be here as it is. So, I'm going to go back to being invisible. Or maybe I should just go back to Ireland. At least there, I won't have to face the pain that fills me anytime I see him. And he'll never find out the truth or my secret I now hold to myself.

The End.

Dear Readers,

Thank you for reading Hellhound's Sacrifice. I hope you enjoyed the rollercoaster of Hellhound and Isabelle. Now, if you're wondering about the Black Clovers, check out A. Gorman's books to meet the rest of the Ryans. For those ready to know about Angel, don't worry, his story is coming up next in the Satan's Keepers MC series. It's set to release this Summer.

Sincerely,

E.C.

War

I'll do anything to keep her safe.

War

I swore I'd never fall for a woman again. Not after the trouble I've been through. They're nothing but a headache. Then I saw her—hopeless and fighting to survive.

Something inside me sparks to life, and now she's mine to protect. I just gotta show her I mean what I say, and I'm not like others. Just as she's showing me, she's not the same as the women in my past.

Breathing in Sin

Aspen

No one said life had a guidebook to help make it through times like now. One that led me to him. If they had, I would have taken a different path altogether. Instead, I struck a deal with him, giving him control over all that is me. Unfortunately, I didn't know my heart would be on the line, same as my next breath as danger came to his door.

Inheriting Trouble

Moving to Norhill Tops seemed like a good idea at the time. She thought it would be the escape she needed. Little did she know it was only more trouble adding up. Does she put her trust in the town and the people in it, especially the hunky sheriff, who seems to think of her as a pain?

Remaining Gunner's

I lost her once, but she remains mine all the same.

Gunner

Years ago, I lost the one woman who held my heart. We were still kids ourselves when it happened. She loved me near as much as I did her, but then she disappeared—no trace to be found. I looked but could never find her.

Now years later, she's back, but a lot has changed in that time. I've got a kid I didn't know about until recently. On top of that, we lost my daughter's mother in a fire.

Tragedy surrounds us, constantly looming. When she stepped into view, I swore she was a figment of my imagination. Then I looked closer. She was real. Worse, she was hurt. I don't know what she's been through. I'll do what it takes to make things right. I lost one woman I cared about. I won't lose the one who claimed my heart.

Available Now

By: E.C. Land

Devil's Riot MC Series

Horse's Bride

Thorn's Revenge

Twister's Survival

Reclaimed (Devil's Riot MC Boxset Bks 1 – 3)

Cleo's Rage

Connors' Devils

Hades Pain

Badger's Claim

Burner's Absolution

Redeemed (Devil's Riot MC Boxset Bks 4 – 6)

K-9's Fight

Devil's Riot MC Originals

Stoney's Property

Owning Victoria

Blaze's Mark

Taming Coyote

Luna's Shadow

Choosing Nerd

Ranger's Fury

Carrying Blaze's Mark

Neo's Strength

Cane's Dominance

Venom's Prize

Devil's Ride (DRMC Boxset 1-5)

Protecting Blaze's Mark

Whip's Breath

Viper's Touch

DRMC Southeast

Hammer's Pride

Malice's Soul

Axe's Devotion

Rebelling Rogue

Ruin Boxset 1-3

DRMC Tennessee

Blow's Smoke

Inferno's Clutch MC

Chains' Trust

Breaker's Fuse

Ryder's Rush

Axel's Promise

Fated for Pitch Black

Tiny's Hope

Their Redemption

Fuse's Hold

Nora's Outrage

Tyres' Wraith

Brielle's Nightmare

Pipe's Burn

Dark Lullabies

A Demon's Sorrow

A Demon's Bliss

A Demon's Harmony

A Demon's Soul

A Demon's Song

Dark Lullabies Boxset

Royal Bastards MC (Elizabeth City Charter)

Cyclone of Chaos

Spiral into Chaos

Aligned Hearts

Embraced

Entwined

Entangled

Ensnared

Crush Boxset 1-3

Night's Bliss

Finley's Adoration (Co-Write with Elizabeth Knox)

Cedric's Ecstasy

Arwen's Rapture

Satan's Keepers MC

Keeping Reaper

Forever Tombstone's

Hellhound's Sacrifice

Toxic Warriors MC

Viking

Ice

De Luca Crime Family

Frozen Valentine (Prequel)

Frozen Kiss

Pins and Needles Series with Elizabeth Knox

Blood and Agony

Blood and Torment

Blood & Betrayal

DeLancy Crime Family with Elizabeth Knox

Degrade

Deprave

Detest

Desire Boxset 1-3

Deny

Raiders of Valhalla with Elizabeth Knox

Malicious

Sinister

Malevolent

Spiteful

Menacing

Deathstalkers MC with Elizabeth Knox

Kinetic

Anthologies

Twisted Steel: Third Edition

Available on Audible

Reclaimed

Cleo's Rage

Connors' Devils

Hades Pain

Badger's Claim

Coming Soon
By: E.C. Land

Devil's Riot MC
Red's Calm

Devil's Riot MC Originals
Cyprus' Truth

DRMC Southeast
Remaining Gunner's

Inferno's Clutch MC
Faith's Tears

Aligned Hearts
Entrapped
Enchanted

Night's Bliss
Christmas Delight
Halton's Pleasure

Satan's Keepers MC
Outrage Boxset 1-3

Toxic Warriors MC

War
Storm Boxset 1-3
Maverick
Grimm
Dice

De Luca Crime Family
Heated Caress

Raiders of Valhalla MC with Elizabeth Knox
Shameful

Deathstalkers MC with Elizabeth Knox
Falcon

DeLancy Crime Family with Elizabeth Knox
Demean

Sons of Norhill Tops
Inheriting Trouble

Breathing in Sin: The Sinful 8 Book 6

Anthologies
Cover Up
The Elites: Year Two

SOCIAL MEDIA
BE SURE TO FOLLOW OR STALK ME!

Goodreads
Bookbub
DRMC BABES
Instagram
Author Page

Printed in Great Britain
by Amazon